Turning the Tide

Whittle's Vampires Book Two

Emily Starr

Published in 2020 by FeedARead.com Publishing

Copyright © Emily Starr
Editing by Gill Shaw-Hogg
Layout Geraldine Ann Ford
Front Cover Shuttlestock

The author or authors assert their moral right under the Copyright, Designs and Patents Act, 1988, to be identified as the author or authors of this work.

All Rights reserved. No part of this publication may be reproduced, copied, stored in a retrieval system, or transmitted, in any form or by any means, without the prior written consent of the copyright holder, nor be otherwise circulated in any form of binding or cover other than that in which it is published and without a similar condition being imposed on the subsequent purchaser.

A CIP catalogue record for this title is available from the British Library.

Westerdale (unavailable)
Rainharrow (unavailable)
Heaton
The Calling
Bleak Spirit (about the Brontes)
Split Moonbeam (the story of my great-grandmother)
Summer Madness
The Awakening
Winter Violet
Gabriel Messenger
Briarly
Whittle's Vampires Book One

All royalties from the sale of this book will be donated to Ty Nant Cat Sanctuary - reg charity 1169025
Website: www.tynantcatsanctuary.org

Ty Nant Cat sanctuary is a not for profit organisation rescuing cats, both feral and domestic, and seeking to rehome them in loving forever homes. They also provide long term care for cats who find it difficult to secure a home through disability, age or temperament.

To all my cats, past, present and future, and my father: I affectionately dedicate this book.

CHAPTER ONE

"I came as soon as I could, Lawrence." Verity's face was drawn and pale in the spring dusk and her hands shook as she pushed her long, dark hair away from her eyes.

Lawrence felt a stab of pain.

Oh God, if I had been with him and not struck down by the fever, then this would not have happened, he thought. Was Frederick careless or are we facing a threat like never before here in these dark, damp valleys?

"Do you know what happened?" Verity was asking now. Lawrence seemed to her like a man in a dream and she had to repeat her question in order to elicit a reply.

"He went alone on his quest," Lawrence told her, "I was indisposed with an ague and shook from head to foot. It was a perilous journey here and I am not as young as I was."

"You thought to give all this up once, I believe," Verity prompted him when silence had fallen.

"I did," he came back with, "I planned on making my home in Scar's End and seeing my days out with kith and kin, a happy man, but Alphonso's death put paid to that."

"What do you mean?" she asked him, putting off the dreadful moment when she would have to see the man she loved.

Lawrence shrugged.

"I don't know but something changed in me that night. I am not the same man I was. To be faced with that evil...bogged down with it, overwhelmed with it and yet, with a single blow, to be able to eradicate it. It makes a man think."

Verity was silent. She could think of nothing further to say and, besides, she was exhausted after the long and rough journey. Wales! She felt dizzy with lack of sleep and her heart raced.

"I knew there was something between you, that much I suspected, long before Alphonso was killed," Lawrence was saying now, "I saw it more on Frederick's side than yours of course, he being my friend and me being very lately acquainted with you."

"I returned that love, Lawrence. There was never any doubt in my mind about that. I may have been confused by what I found at Scar's End but as for my feelings, they were crystal clear. I love him."

Lawrence shook his head,

"You loved him," he replied loudly, "Loved. You cannot love what is left to us. I called you here to see what this affliction has reduced him to. By day he prays for me to kill him but at night he seeks my death, my blood. You cannot love a vampire. You know what that will do to him."

"So, how am I to face him when this love in my heart will not go away, try as I might to extinguish it?"

"You will not face him. At least, not directly. You can view his suffering from behind the screen I have made and then you must go back to Scar's End and get on with your life."

Verity was appalled and now it was her turn to shake her head.

"I cannot do that," she said, "You cannot ask me to be so cruel and heartless. There has to be another way."

Lawrence grabbed her arm and shook her.

"Open your eyes, Miss Whittle. Open your eyes. This is not Frederick and were you to see him when darkness covers his face, you would be as terrified as I am. This is the wreck of a man left behind after the vampire drained him..."

"I suppose he is lucky to be alive," interrupted Verity, jumping when Lawrence threw back his head and laughed long and loud at her words.

"Lucky?" he cried, "Oh yes, very lucky. A poacher found him early the next morning with the marks of the devil in his neck and brought him to me, more dead than alive. More Undead. If he had left this life for one of eternal wandering you would not be standing there, Miss Whittle!"

"Verity, please," cried the distressed woman, "It makes it sound so...," she struggled for words.

"Formal? Serious? Do you realise what I am faced with if I do not stake him, Verity? He will outlive me and predate. I cannot sleep a wink at night for fear he escapes."
"You have him secured then?"
"For now," replied Lawrence, calming a little as he saw Verity had grasped the situation at last, "This place is an old monastery with only twelve brothers calling it home and one of them a good friend of mine. They agreed to take the man...if I should call him that...and hide him away provided I cared for him, which I do. It is no labour of love when he is screaming out for blood but no-one hears him except me, as we have the west wing all to ourselves and, yes, what is left of Frederick makes delightful company! If he escapes then we are all done for."
"Does he know what has happened to him?" asked Verity, wiping away some tears with her gloves.
"Yes, in daylight hours he is fairly lucid and begs me to free him, which of course, I cannot do. He even looks like the old Frederick, although there is the mark of the devil still on his neck. At night, he seeks one thing...blood."
"Do you give it to him?"
  Lawrence laughed.
"Oh yes," he smiled, "The monks have their own animals here and only by sacrificing them can I get any peace."
  Verity shuddered. She had never been easy with eating living flesh and had insisted, when quite a small child, that no animal should be slaughtered for her plate.
That is not the Frederick I know, she thought and her heart was heavy with sorrow. She had expected to be his wife and face the demons they chased together but she knew now such dreams were just that...dreams. She had lost him.

  Down, down, down dark, damp steps, so that Verity thought for a moment that Lawrence had lost his way in this maze of corridors and cold stone. His footsteps carried on, squelching on slimy, wet stairs that seemed to be leading to the bowels of the earth but she paused and listened to the chant of voices above them. Evensong possibly and darkness on its way. Lawrence must have sensed her hesitancy as he called her to hurry; the light was leaving the sky and soon, it would be too dangerous for her to see Frederick. She descended once more but her heart beat so fast that she thought it would explode.

Another flight of stone steps and then they were in a high tunnel leading to the left and Lawrence raised his lantern and bid her wait there whilst he unfolded the screen for her. She heard a low growling, like an animal in pain and her thoughts sped to Jet, left behind and in Liddy's erratic care.

Lawrence returned and Verity asked him,
"That noise...I heard it...is it..."
"Yes," interrupted Lawrence, "He is changing and we have but minutes before you must ascend and seek accommodation with the monks before returning home. Hurry and follow me."

She ran to keep up with the man and came to a folded wooden screen with part of a panel cut out so that she could look through. Lawrence beckoned her to step forward and, after pulling the screen around her, she heard him draw off. The lantern was hung on a hook at the top of the screen and she could see fairly clearly through the two inch gap. A sharp noise, like the sound of nails on stone, greeted her ears as she applied her eyes to the viewing hole.

It took her eyes a while to get used to the lack of light but, during that time, she could see the bars of a cage, a massive prison of rusted metal and, hanging in that prison, chains, coming down from the walls. Soon, her sight adjusted to focus on a man, a rather gaunt figure, who seemed to be sharpening his nails on the bare stone wall behind him. She gave a gasp as she recognised the figure and the creature turned at her exclamation, so she had a good view of him. There was no doubt it was Frederick.

The man was becoming increasingly agitated as night drew near and she observed him pacing up and down and uttering, every so often, a deep groan. Frederick! At least he was still alive! Yet in her heart of hearts she knew this was no life and every word Lawrence said was true. She could not love him,

not because he had turned into this blood-lusting creature, but because her love would strangle and destroy him.
"There has to be a way out of this," she whispered to herself, but she knew Frederick had heard her as he pressed his face against the bars and called out,
"Who is there?"
Her heart sought to answer him and her lips framed words but, suddenly, Lawrence was upon her and had clapped his hand hard over her mouth.
"You cannot talk to him," he whispered fiercely, "I told you no contact of any kind. Can you not see how mad he is becoming and soon, his screams will echo out until dawn penetrates these gloomy dungeons? Do not make my task any harder than it already is! Come with me now!"
"Just one more look," she whispered and applied her eyes to the hole once more.

Frederick was standing by the locked door, his ears listening for any sound and she knew he felt her presence there, even though she was now surrounded by silence. Her heart bled for the man she loved, alas, man no more and she saw the wild, blood-flecked whites of his eyes and his hair that had grown long and unkempt, even though it had only been a few weeks since she saw him last.
Would she ever see him again, she wondered? Or was he doomed to wander through her nightmares like some restless spirit, until Lawrence grew tired of caring for him and put a stake through his heart?

Lawrence, at length, pulled her back and, taking her arm, led her away and up, up, up to where the chanting continued and the air was purer. Reaching a room Lawrence referred to as the refectory, they stopped and Verity sunk into a carved wooden chair. A small fire was burning even though it was a warm evening but the all-pervading damp of the place made Verity shiver.
"I never thought it would end like this," she murmured when Lawrence brought her some bread and wine.
"You concur that it is over then?" he asked.
"For now," she admitted, bowing her head.

They sat down at the table together and ate a silent meal. During her simple repast, Verity studied her companion and thought he had aged greatly since she saw him last. His thin shoulders were bowed and he looked like a beaten man with dull eyes and a heavy heart.

"So when will you end it for...for...Frederick?" she asked when he had cleared the plates and goblets away. She found it hard to say her love's name and her voice shook with emotion.

"When I find I cannot cope with it any more," replied Lawrence shortly, wondering if he had done the right thing in summoning Verity here.

"Will you tell me?"

Lawrence sighed.

"I see no benefit in letting you know," he told her.

"But should I not be here to pray for him?" she asked tearfully.

"The monks will do that. It is their job and way of life."

"You think he has forgotten me?"

"No, he mentions you in more lucid moments but he knows and understands that he will never see you or be your husband."

Verity bit her lip.

"So you want me to leave here tomorrow and never look back? You think I can be that heartless?"

"You have to be. There is no choice."

"But what if there was a way..."

Lawrence slapped his open hand down upon the table with some force.

"There is no way," he informed her, "Only the stake...only the mallet. You have seen it and you know the truth. When you sleep here tonight you must send him just enough love to keep him away."

"But not enough to kill him?"

Lawrence shrugged.

"Far better that he went, strangled with the love I see shining in your eyes, than with a bloody stake through his heart, fighting me with every inch of his strength."

"You want me to murder him with my love? I cannot do that but I cannot hate him either or have fear for his state. I remember him as kind, caring and loyal."

"Then leave here tomorrow with that image of him in your heart and keep it there as a pleasant memory in the years that follow."

Long, empty years, thought Verity. How can I ever love again with this emotion filling my heart?

"I must leave you now," Lawrence told her when he saw she had no further questions for him, "I must keep watch over Frederick and he will want feeding."

Verity shuddered. A life slaughtered to feed another life. It was so wrong. Blood to feed the blood lust.

"My friend will come in soon to eat bread and drink wine and he will show you to your room," Lawrence told her.

"So I shall see you no more tonight?" she asked.

"No."

She could hear him praying as he left, even though his words were low.

"Dear God, this very night, give me the strength to get through whatever may come my way and bring me to the new dawn thankful and alive..."

A click of the heavy wooden door and he was gone.

"Goodnight," she called out but darkness had closed over him and she saw him no more. She returned to the fire and waited for the monks to finish their ministrations.

Sleep, she thought, even with exhaustion overcoming my body, is far from my mind. Every turn of the carriage wheels tomorrow takes me further and further away from the man that I love. Should I go or stand and fight and, if I do fight, where are my weapons? What weapons can you use against a vampire, or one turned into a vampire by the poison injected into his veins?

She was deep in thought when the door swung open once more and the tall figure of a monk entered.

"Miss Whittle, I wish you good evening. I have come to show you to your room. I am Curlious, Adam Curlious, long time friend of Lawrence Grey."

Verity bowed her head and left her sad reverie behind.
"Thank you, Mr Curlious. I am beholden to you for your hospitality."
"It is under very sad circumstances, Miss Whittle. I know a little of your history and it is, indeed, a tragic one."

Verity felt a sudden bond with this man and she knew, instantly, that she could trust him. They were both young, even though he had huge dark circles under his eyes, which spoke of sleepless nights and utter devotion to the God he served. He was quiet, he was sincere and who better than a brother of the cloth to open your soul to?
"Do you have to be somewhere, Mr Curlious, in the next few minutes? I mean, I hesitate to take up even a second of your time knowing your vocation..."
"My time is my own, Miss, once evening prayers are said."
"I heard your singing and chanting and it moved me to tears," she admitted.

The monk acknowledged her compliment with a bow.
"Let us sit down," he said, "and I will see if I can help you. That is, if you want or need my help and if there is any way I can assist you, of course."

Verity went back to her wooden chair by the dying fire and the monk took one opposite her and heaped wood on the embers so they roared back into life again. He settled himself comfortably and asked her again what ailed her.
"You know a little of my history, I take it?" she began cautiously, feeling that she was burdening an already troubled man. Something in the shine of those eyes told her Curlious had suffered too and maybe that was why he had sought sanctuary in the habit. Her sixth sense had picked up a kindred spirit and she knew she would be listened to with warmth and dignity. Lawrence was already out of his depths and the task he faced alone left him little energy for listening to problems of any kind.
"You are aware, I take it, that I met Lawrence very recently in Scar's End in northern England, just on the edge of Hanworth Moor. He came to me because the house I inherited from my uncle was the focus of vampires and his

friend Frederick, who now exists...I will not say lives...in the cellars of your west wing, was a vampire hunter."

The monk nodded at this.

"I had heard this much," he admitted, "Also that your uncle was one of the Undead and sought you out for company in the eternal world of darkness these creatures inhabit."

"You know a little about vampires then, Mr Curlious?"

"Call me Adam, or Brother Adam, as they do here," he told her, "We do not stand on ceremony and we are family once you join the brotherhood. There were some here who did not want a woman in their midst, I must be honest, but to me that is old fashioned and not the way God would want it."

Verity sensed that this monk and Lawrence had pleaded her case and it was because of this quiet, grave man that she was sitting here now. Maybe it had taken them a while to persuade the Father to let her visit but at least she was here and it was not too late. Frederick was alive, at least.

"You are familiar with vampire lore then, Brother Adam," she repeated.

He nodded his head at this and mentioned that his father was from Transylvania, although he, himself, had been born in this country.

"Your father is still alive, I take it?" she asked.

"He is. A hermit in the mountains of South Wales but very much alive and serving his God in splendid isolation!"

She understood a little more and pushed on with her story.

"Frederick and Lawrence killed all the vampires in my corner of the world and it was a very hard task, for the Master, who controlled them, put up such a fight as I have never seen a living soul put up before..."

"But we must remember they are not living, Miss Whittle. They are certainly Undead and as such, have the strength of the Devil in their hearts."

"That is so, Adam, and in the end, whilst Lawrence and Frederick grappled with the vampire, I had to stake him. It has troubled me ever since, that I killed a man. I murdered him."

Adam's eyes remained calm.

"How could that be, since he was never really alive to begin with?" he asked, "He was dead and doomed when the first bite came upon him and you had no control over that!"

"You do not think badly of me then?" she queried, "You are a man of God and as such, are here to save and protect life."

"That is so," Adam acknowledged, "However, you sent a suffering soul into the arms of that God, so how can you look upon it as anything but a kind act?"

Verity was moved to smile.

"I do not think Alphonso saw it that way," she admitted, "However, you have eased my troubled heart with your words."

"Is that all that is troubling you?" he asked her when a full minute of silence had ensued.

At this she shook her head.

"No," she said, "My heartache is the man who is in your cellar, craving fresh blood and ripping your animals apart just to exist. He is my betrothed."

Adam nodded his head.

"I had heard from Lawrence that there was an understanding between the two of you before Frederick came to help us here."

Verity looked around her.

"So you have vampires here, in the monastery?" she asked in surprise.

Adam shook his head.

"We serve the local village," he said, "The settlement you may have seen as your carriage drew up, nothing but a stone's throw from this place. They have problems with these bloodsuckers and after a child was taken, we could wait no longer and so sent for your...fiancé, shall I say?"

"Yes," agreed Verity, "For he left me a ring and a promise."

"Now broken I take it and lost forever?"

Adam's eyes were calm and his countenance demure, like a blank canvas, but that did not fool Verity.

"The promise is only broken by HIS affliction," she admitted, "In MY heart it stands as strong and as unyielding as it ever did."

Adam did not reply for a moment and she knew he was deep in thought. At length he nodded and asked her what she would do to claim Frederick from the dark forces that held him.

"For he is lost in a mist that is neither death nor life but an eternal wandering, without a soul. Yet his soul is not in heaven and neither is it in hell but it resides in some 'no-man's land', waiting for redemption. His heart is there too and, when freed from the box it inhabits, it could yet destroy the curse that is placed upon him."

"You know a lot, Adam, and you see a lot. Your eyes have seen a man bitten by a vampire before, I can tell."

"That is true," he acknowledged.

Verity grew excited and leaned forward in her seat.

"There are cures...herbs, potions, medicines?" she asked breathlessly.

"He already has those and they keep him relatively quiet during the hours of darkness, once his blood lust has been fed."

"Then what, Adam, what? For I feel someone close to you has survived the bite from a vampire? Your eyes speak volumes but your tongue is silent, as if you will offend me by telling all."

"It is a long, hard road, Miss Whittle, and one you must travel alone, were you to take up the gauntlet. Or, you could just return to Scar's End and get on with your life."

"You really think I could do that?"

He shook his head.

"But you could die trying to save him," he warned her.

"Better to die trying than to return to an existence of pain and misery, ill-nourished by tragic memories and haunted constantly by what might have been," she told him, "Please tell me, I must know of what you speak. I take it the Reverend Father would not approve of your words and they are not ones to be uttered in a holy building."

"No."

She nodded her head. A small but definite ray of light had appeared on the horizon and she had to press on before this illumination vanished.

"What is it?" she whispered, "Adam, I have to know what I must prepare myself for before I set out on this long, hard road as you call it."

"Witchcraft," he said quietly. He then folded his hands and would say no more.

CHAPTER TWO

Into her subconscious mind, Frederick entered and suddenly, the sweet sleep Verity was experiencing fled like shadows before the sun. Her heart began to beat fast and her eyelids, though closed, flickered and half opened. Where was she?

Calming, she returned to the land of sleep but her dreams were destined to be nightmares now that her beloved was inside her head.

"Verity...Verity...why will you not come to me? We are betrothed and, as such, your life is mine. Offer me your neck..."

Verity writhed and squirmed on her pillow.

"No, no," came her answer, "I cannot surrender myself to you, Frederick. You have been bitten by a vampire and there is a wall between us!"

"Then help me knock it down! Mere bricks between us...that will not stop us..."

"It cannot be, Frederick. I am strong, I am resilient. Do not make me send you the love I feel for you in my heart. It will bend and break you. Remember Richard? I almost killed him with my affection so please, please do not make me use this pure emotion...I will...I will..."

She sensed he had retreated a little but he was still there, inside her head, and she had to drive him out.

"Please go, Frederick, go. I know you live in torment but I can help you. I can help you. Leave me in the peace I need to be able to end all this..."

She was beginning to release the love in her heart and she knew it would strangle him but no matter how she tried to stifle it the emotion poured forth. She saw him choking and crying but he drew off and, just as suddenly as he came, he was gone.

A cry must have escaped from her lips as she heard a banging at her door and rising from the bed, she flung a shawl around her shoulders and asked who was there.

"Lawrence," came the answer, "Are you hurt? Were you visited?"

She flung the door open to face the man and saw fear in his dark eyes.

"Yes," she said, "He was here, in my head, trying to make me let him in."

"You resisted him?"

"Yes, I sent him love but only enough to repel him."

"Ah, that is why he lies moaning and gasping in his cell. He has been agitated all night because you are here. Come morning light you must go."

The ring of footsteps on stone and the man was gone. Verity watched him draw off down the corridor and, suddenly, the last vestiges of light in the raven black sky disappeared and she despaired.

It was three hours later and sleep had deserted Verity for the night but as the clock struck five, she heard the monks walking to the chapel, chanting as they went, of their love for God. It gave her hope and, besides, in early May, the dawn was coming and with it a time for action.
I will not leave here until I have done all I can to save Frederick, she thought as the monks began their morning songs. So beautiful were their voices that she dressed and slipped out of her room to listen.

Leaning against the door of the chapel, she bathed herself in their music and tried to forget, for a moment, the creature in the west wing cellar that had once been Frederick. She heard them closing in prayer and making plans to leave and, hiding herself under a fall of arras on an adjoining wall, she peered out to see if Adam was among them.

The Reverend Father came out first, followed by two of the more senior monks, and then a couple of young boys, obviously just entering the brotherhood and then, last of all, walked Adam. She waited until he had passed her, then called out to him, as loudly as she dared, hoping the other monks would not hear. He turned at once and saw her and, leaving the procession, he came to her side.

She saw the questions in his eyes and asked him if he could talk more about what was mentioned last night.

"As I have thought of nothing else all night and my dreams have been nightmares."

Adam looked pensive.

"He came to you then," he acknowledged, "Did you have the power to resist him?"

"Yes. I sent him enough love to close his throat and suppress his low vibration but I must have cried out and Lawrence came and told me I must leave today. How can I leave, knowing there is a way to save the man I love?" She sounded desperate and she was but Adam was not happy.

"I should not have said anything," he admitted, "Then you would have gone home none the wiser. Forget my words, Miss Whittle, the road I paint is not for you!"

He was about to turn away but she grabbed his arm and pleaded with him to at least tell her more so she could make up her own mind.

"You may be right, I may not be able to release Frederick from this dreadful affliction, but at least let me try!"

Adam was confused.

"I should not be seen with you," he said, "It is against the laws of the brotherhood, being alone with a woman."

"Then tell me outside the monastery where no such laws impede our speech!" she begged, "I can meet you in the gardens or, beyond that, on the road to the village. I know there is so much more for me to learn concerning this, Adam, and I will not quit this place until I have listened to this information and made up my mind."

Adam sighed.

"You have to understand that even if I wanted to I could not go with you," he told her, "You must go alone and the road is paved with tricksters and demons. Can you avoid them, can you overcome them?"

"Yes, if there is a way," replied Verity, trying to give off a confidence she did not feel, "Have you forgotten I staked a vampire, all by myself, and that creature high up in the hierarchy and all the time pleading for mercy?"

"You fainted afterwards, so Lawrence said," Adam told her. "Meet me, please. Later, but not too late, as Lawrence means to pack me off on a coach this afternoon. He will not allow me to stay."

"The Reverend Father says the same," Adam told her, "He vowed you should not come and one night was all I could persuade him to accept. You were supposed to keep away from us, me included, but Lawrence asked me to show you to your room, which I dutifully did."

"You did far more than that, Adam, and you know it. You planted a seed of hope in my heart and overnight it has grown into a tree!"

"Beware of it, Miss Whittle, that is what I would say to you! It is a poisonous weed and may strangle you as you sleep. It gives you false hope and when you hear the rest of the story you will go back to Scar's End and think of the plan no more!"

"Then I am to hear the rest of it! You promise to meet me?"

"Yes," he said, feeling he had no choice and anxious to be off, "For now, I must go, as I am responsible for the boys and I have to read the Grace before breakfast too. They will notice if I delay any further. Meet me under the big oak, the last tree on our land, where the gate to the monastery lies open and joins the village road. Meet me there in two hours and say nothing to anyone, even Lawrence."

He shook her encircling arm away and, like a leaf in the breeze, was gone.

It is as though he is ethereal, thought Verity, and moves on winged feet but I must not leave here until the whole picture is put before me. Who knows what I can achieve with love on my side?

She went back to her room and waited and, presently, Lawrence brought her breakfast and told her he was going to sleep as Frederick was drugged and resting peacefully.

"The coach comes in three hours," he told her, looking careworn and old, "Be on it, Verity. I shall be awake by then and see that you are. You cannot stay here. This is no place for you and besides, there is nothing further you can do. You have seen the whole, sorry picture with your own eyes and those eyes must now return to Scar's End and seek out another life that does not include Frederick."

Verity said nothing but ate some bread and drank some strange concoction that the monks brewed as tea. She listened to the clock chiming and knew she had but an hour to wait to meet Adam and then decide if she could accept the challenge he was going to put before her.

Have I a choice? said her heart. Keep out of danger, said her head.

She walked about in her room and hoped that Lawrence would not come to see her and it seemed the man slept as no footsteps came her way and the long, austere corridor was silent. She flung on her cloak and, taking her bag with her so that Lawrence would think she had gone if he came to find her, she took a last look and then kissed the cold stone of the buttresses outside her tiny room.

"I don't neglect you, my darling, but I must go to search for a cure so we can be together again," she whispered.

Back came the answer that chilled her soul...

"Ah, but we could be together on the shores of eternity with just one bite...just one bite..."

She shuddered and, driving Frederick's voice from her mind, left the monastery and sought the refuge of the giant oak.

The ancient tree must have been hundreds of years old and as Verity stood there, feeling the chill spring breeze wind round her like a caress, she was aware of the illicit meetings and confrontations the huge oak must have witnessed.

"And you have been silent all these years so that those imparting their heartfelt secrets knew they could trust your sagacity," she told the mottled trunk, as she ran her hand over the rough texture.

"What have you seen I wonder? Generations coming and going, murders...lovers trysts and those destined to die in duels, such as my brother. Yet all of them have gone on to their fate and you have not so much as rattled a leaf to warn them! Do I stand here but briefly and then go on to my death, I wonder? I have no fear, I would rather die trying than commit Frederick to eternal damnation or else a place at Abraham's bosom. Would we then be together at the gates of heaven, I wonder? Perhaps I would be let through and you, dear Frederick, would be sent to where the fire of brimstone burns forever more! Oh I cannot bear to think of that!"

Turning abruptly, she almost knocked Adam over and he raised his eyebrows.

"Talking to trees, Miss Whittle? Happen you get more sense out of them than humans."

"My father taught me to love all of Nature, Adam, and I do," she replied, by way of explanation.

"I noticed you shunned the meat put upon your plate earlier," he acknowledged.

"That was once alive," she told him emotionally, "I will not have the innocent die for my sake and cause so much suffering when I do not need to partake of flesh! I will not eat that suffering and take it into my body when vegetables and fruit are just as nourishing. Do you realise, Adam, that you cannot truly be a man of God when animals, rare and precious lives, are killed for you? Why, it is murder, cold-blooded murder, and something that man should be sent to the Devil for…and fish too, they have feelings and experience pain. A hook through your mouth, Adam, would you like that?"

Verity had drawn herself up to her full height and her dark eyes flashed fire. Adam put his hand up and told her to stop.

"You have proved yourself, completely, in my eyes," he told her, "I have no doubt after witnessing that blazing fire in your talk and seeing it smouldering in your heart. My mind is made up on those few sentences, spoken with such zeal and passion."

Verity was confused.

"Adam," she said simply, having calmed now her mind was on a different track, "Adam, what are you talking about?"

"The quest, the riddle, the recipe, if you could call it that. You have the power and the fight to undertake what I did a few years ago for my father. Draw closer and let us sit on this beautiful and peaceful tree. Sadly, the things we have to talk about are neither of those things but they could bring you fulfilment and freedom. I will set the very spells and potions I experienced before you, Miss Whittle, and you must then decide if you will use that strong spirit to go and collect them."

It was two hours later and Verity walked with Adam to visit his father, with whom the monk said Verity could stay whilst pondering over the proposal, if she needed to. Verity's head was a-whirl with what she had lately heard and part of her was still incredulous.
"Dragons, Adam? Dragons?" she said in a whisper, so profound was the effect of his words upon her, "It sounds just like a fairy tale and I, a naughty child, refusing to sleep. Like a story that is there, lurking, in the dark recesses of your imagination."
Adam nodded.
"I feared you would say this," he replied, "Hence why we are on the way to visit my father, high on the mountainside. Maybe when you hear it from his lips too, you will believe."
"I have to believe, don't I Adam, if I am to succeed."
"Yes, Verity, there is that. Let one crumb of doubt enter your head and you are done for. The plan will not come to fruition."
"So love and faith are an important part of this?"
"I would say they are the most vital part," Adam told her, "Without them you have failed before you have taken one step to save Frederick."
Verity nodded but her heart sank. How could she believe in a fable? Dragons dwelling in the Welsh valleys? How could that be? She was very troubled but now needed all her strength and attention to climb the steep path before her up the mountain. Adam, she noted, was as sure-footed as one of the mountain goats they had lately passed on the winding path. Her breath came in pants and she acknowledged to Adam that, though she was young, she was not as fit as he.

"I come every week to bring my father food and wine," the monk told her, "Thus, I am used to the steepness of the path; in fact, it can be worse on the descent if slippery with rain or fallen scree."

"Will I be coming back?" asked Verity, more to herself than to her companion and he, perceiving the question was not for him, declined to answer.

"It will be a very, very difficult road you tread, Miss Whittle, should you decide to take up the reins and ride the wild horse of magic but you can end this affliction. You must think of it as though Frederick has been cursed with a black spell and you are out to release him."

"The witch you told me about, she will help me with that? A full five years ago you faced what I do now, so how can you be sure that the creatures you visited are still alive and willing to assist me?"

"I did not say they were willing to help you, Miss Whittle. That part you must work out for yourself. Surely, they will respond differently to you than they did to me. Bring them what they ask for and all will be well. Besides, dragons live forever," he finished, sensing she doubted his words.

She did not reply to this, so jumbled were her thoughts and, as they reached the summit and a number of caves appeared, she knew she must prepare herself to pose the most important questions of her life to a man she had never met. Her heart almost failed her, as she had never been a social creature, but the fact that Adam was with her gave her some courage, at least. If only he could go with her on her journey!

The last cave was the biggest and Adam plunged into it, calling for his father, and receiving a distant reply. Verity remained where she was but presently, the monk bid her to enter and presented his father who carried a large staff and was clad in a simple sacking outfit from head to toes. He stepped forward into the light and announced that he was delighted to meet her.

Verity hurried forward and took his offered hand which was warm and smelt of herbs and salve. Turning to behold him clearer, she sought his face and noticed at once that he had no eyes. The man was blind.

CHAPTER THREE

There was a poignant silence in the cave for a moment and then the old man began to speak.
"Come forward child and take a seat, for I see you have a heavy and troubled heart."
Verity felt very awkward.
"How...how can you tell that?" she stammered, making for the slab of rock that Adam covered with a sack in order to protect her clothing.
"Ah," said the hermit, "You think that because I have no outer eyes I do not perceive things and that people are but wandering shapes to me? Credit me with more intelligence, Miss Whittle, for I once had orbs as dark and tearful as your own. In my mind I still have them and therefore I can tune in to emotion and so much more when people surround me. You are fearful and sad but the tragedy in your life can be lifted. It can be lifted with faith."
Verity was amazed at his comments but her tongue kept silent whilst he began his story.
"I am an old man, Miss Whittle, but it was not always so. Once I was married to Adam's beautiful mother and my children sat with me, night after night. They grew up strong and healthy but then the fever came and took my wife and after her, my daughter. It was then that the vampires crossed my path here and I knew nothing of turning the tide, as I call it, nothing of witchcraft or dragons or spells. Yes, I used herbs as a holy man, but I made no incantations over them and God was the only one I worshipped."
"You saw then? You had eyes?" asked Verity, feeling she was being rude in naming the sense he had lost.
"Oh, yes, I had eyes as huge and limpid as Adam's. Even now I feel them gazing at me, although that is only in my soul, Miss Whittle, in my heart. I lost my eyes when I challenged the vampire law and Adam caused the moon and the stars to turn the tide and bring new life to the Undead.

For what is there but death when you are Undead? Now you know the secret...there is life."

"I have told her my story, Father, but I sense doubts in her heart and fear in her soul."

The old man nodded his head.

"Yes," he agreed, "I sense it too and it comes across with a bitter, suffocating air, Miss Whittle. Can you calm it? Can you rip it from your life and replace it with hope and faith instead? For they will win you the prize."

"My fiancé was bitten by one of these bloodsuckers when he first came to this land," Verity told him, "He is caged like a wild animal and fed, in order that I may undertake this trial and bring light to the darkness in which he presently exists. He is Undead but if there is a chance of him living, however small, then I have to take it." She sounded confident but she did not feel it.

"Yet doubts persist," acknowledged the old man.

"Yes, Mr Curlious, and they rankle," she admitted, "How do I evict them from a mind that has long been used to dealing with reality and facts?"

The hermit shook his head.

"That I cannot tell you," he said, "The road you must travel has demons on every side waiting for such doubts and if you hesitate, Miss Whittle, you are lost."

"Yet your son had such faith, Mr Curlious, and he set out alone along that road. He reached the end and now you stand restored before me."

"True, but he is a man of God."

"So you think me a heathen who has never had a Bible in my hand? Why, I used that Holy Book to repel my uncle and finally bring him to his knees a few months ago. I praised God then and I praise Him now, as I know He saved me. So, is it my faith in God that will save me, as I wander this lonely road?"

"No," said the old man, "It is your faith in yourself that will bring you to the end triumphant. There is a fire in you I see, Miss Whittle, and it burns bright but material things may rise up and extinguish it. Is the love you feel for this man…what was his name?"

"Frederick," she retorted, feeling some hope in saying the name.

"Frederick," continued the hermit, "I ask you…is this love strong enough to see you round the dark and dangerous corners of this road?"

Verity allowed herself to feel the full force of that love but knew she must hide it from Frederick, lest it destroy him. "It is," she said firmly, "It is the all-encompassing force in my life and it directs my every thought and my every action."

The old man nodded and smiled, as though he approved of what he had heard. He sat down on a rocky ledge and resumed his story.

"I was born in Transylvania, Miss Whittle, and there, vampires are a very unpleasant pest, much as people here complain about foxes and black crows..."

"I don't!" interjected Verity, with some spirit, "They have the right to live, the same as the rest of us. Why shoot them and then hang their poor, bedraggled corpses from trees, as if to say that man has power over them? He does NOT! Nature is her own goddess and very beautifully she fits every animal and bird into creation. You say you worship God, Mr Curlious, well I say I worship Nature and every creature in it!"

The old man smiled.

"I like your spirit, Miss Whittle, I like it very much and it will serve you when the road is dark and rocky! However, I must ask you if you feel that vampires are part of this creation you talk about loving? Does your regard extend to the bloodsuckers, for surely they are part of this tree of life at whose roots you worship?"

"I abhor them as much as I love the natural world," came the answer, "They are an abomination to the Nature I love! Why, they predate on it! The number of sheep they ripped to pieces night after night, on the moors where I live, because they could get no human blood, appalled me! I killed one of their masters, only a few weeks ago and I was glad I did it, after the initial shock passed over me."

The hermit clapped his hands together.
"Why you have spirit, Miss Whittle, I must say and you will need that spirit for the long road ahead. I am not surprised that my son saw you as a fit contender to attempt the maze you must travel through if you are to release your loved one from his affliction. However, I have lost my thread and we must pull my story together if you are to understand exactly what you face. Adam has told you of his journey?"
"Yes, and there were doubts in my mind concerning it, I will allow, but I am overcoming these doubts since I spoke to you, Mr Curlious."
"Good, good," he replied, "Adam, we forget our manners and must offer Miss Whittle some refreshment. Do you wish to keep a clear head, my dear, and drink of the herbs I concoct or is the wine Adam brings more to your liking?"

Verity desired nothing more than water and the old man took a goblet of wine whilst Adam drank a strange green tea that he said would give him the strength to tackle the long descent back to the monastery.
"As I said, Miss Whittle, I was born in the very region that gave birth to these monsters and we never went far from home in case we met them on the road. Garlic and crucifixes were what we carried and a mirror, for they cast no reflection, as you possibly know. We were brought up with these devils in our midst and, yes, they predated on us if they could, but very often every door and window was closed to them and we learnt from a young age not to walk about at night. Occasionally a traveller was found with his throat ripped out or, if the vampire did a neater job, the tell-tale marks of two teeth, deep in the flesh. Sometimes they were alive and sometimes dead...or Undead, as I should of course say, and many were the vampire hunters we had in our country, trying to rid our lanes of these demons. We never quite succeeded. Oh yes, for many moons only the odd one came to our door disguised as a lost child but Mother was

never fooled and Father would not even open the door so we were safe, after a fashion.

Time went on, Miss Whittle, and both my parents died of old age and an opportunity came for me to come to England aboard a ship, as the companion of a wealthy businessman who was introduced to me by my uncle. He was a strange man, dark and secretive, but he required my help to restore an old manor house he had inherited in the depths of Wales. I had become very proficient in designing and building dwellings, you see.

The trip from my native land was fraught with danger as the seas were rough and several souls perished, their bodies thrown overboard so their grieving relations could not see what they died of. I remained healthy and we came into harbour here with just four of the original crew intact. What the others died from, Miss Whittle, I did not know.

For several years I worked on the Welsh manor house, building different rooms and enlarging it, always enlarging it, for many were the guests my employer, a Mr Raven, had to stay. He had me build myself a small cottage in the grounds when I fell in love with Adam's mother, and thus we lived and raised two children. Yet Mr Raven did not change. After twenty years the lines of time did not bead his face and neither did the grey of age adorn his hair. People talked about it, oh yes, but they did not cross him. Those that crossed him...vanished.

He only asked one thing of me, in all those years, and that was to stay in when the moon was high and darkness covered the sky with her cloak and, although I thought it odd, I did his bidding as he paid me well and we lived a good life. Where his wealth came from I did not know, nor did I care as long as my wages were forthcoming every week. However, many other Welsh peasants and farmers did not feel so easy with the man and he was not generally liked. I got used to his rough, curt manner and the fact that he often slept in till past midday. I knew my duties and I stuck to them but one day, when dusk was just sweeping over the sky and I was making my way home before darkness fell, I met a young woman who told me she had been out in the woods last night and had seen a creature with burning red eyes, draining the blood from a dead deer. She was adamant that she had watched the thing and it had turned into a bat in front of her eyes and flown off.

Instantly, my guard was up and the past was dissolved as I recognised the telltale marks of a vampire. Had this girl imagined all she saw or was it a nightmare? I decided to slip out later and return to the spot to see if I could see through her eyes, as it was. I had garlic and my crucifix on me and the night was dark and cold but I knew, for my own sanity, I had to find out what lurked in the woods at night.

For three nights I waited and saw only deer and a fox but on the fourth night, as I was committing her words to the realms of fantasy, I heard the sound of bony wings and down to the forest clearing came one of the creatures I had seen as a child, in my homeland. The vampire searched the naked trees; it was January then, Miss Whittle, and I feared it had smelt my blood but I stayed put and, eventually, it seemed to give up its quest and, returning to the form of a bat, it flew off. I endeavoured to follow it and found it feeding on a fresh deer carcass only a stone's throw from Harlian House, where my employer lived. By now my fear had been overcome and, seeking to ascertain just who this thing was, I crept from the shadows and caught a glimpse of the creature as it wiped the blood from its mouth and made to leave its meal.

I gasped aloud with shock as I recognised Mr Raven, the very man I had accompanied to this land all those years ago. He heard my gasp and knew I had recognised him. A tussle ensued, Miss Whittle, but I got away and my family and I ran through the night to escape his reign of terror. We came south to this part of Wales and found both work and accommodation but the fear of him finding me was always in my heart. I knew he was immortal and whilst I aged and grew weak he did not.

Sadly, my wife sank to rest, as I told you, and is buried but a few feet from here and my daughter, too, died of the fever that took her and thus only Adam and I were left. I tried to throw myself into my work and when Adam told me he wanted to take Holy Orders I was not against it, as I thought it would offer some protection to him, should Mr Raven come after us. However, years had passed and my guard was let down. I persuaded myself that the creature could have been destroyed and be at God's right hand, where repentant sinners may sit, or he could be deep in the bowels of hell. I knew that by Mr Raven's means these bloodsuckers had come to the Welsh valleys and spread out, and I heard, over the course of time, stories of encounters with these demons and always the locations getting closer and closer; nearer and nearer.

On Halloween I always felt the world of the spirits was around us, whether for good or evil, and as such I made sure Adam was safe; but a few years ago, when I was walking by the river on just such a date, I noticed a beautiful woman struggling with a large bag and, as it was daylight, I approached her and offered help. She told me she was carrying the bag to the next village and, as that was my path, I offered to go with her and carry the load.

At the next village she told me she had further to go and at the next and the next and suddenly, it was dark, I was alone with her and fear weighed heavily on my heart. I told her I could help her no more but she insisted just another few steps and we went on and on and on.

Resting against a boulder with the load by my left shoulder, I fell asleep and dreamed such a nightmare of vampires and ghouls and witches that I screamed aloud for deliverance from the torment. Worse was to follow as, when I opened my eyes, no beautiful maiden did I see but a pair of red eyes glaring down at me and the foul stench of a vampire's breath.

I struggled with the demon for many a minute, Miss Whittle, and I knew it was Mr Raven, come back to take his revenge for my betrayal of him and for walking the forest by night, all those years ago. He brought the cunning of the fox and the power of the bear to the fight and, at last, I was overcome and he bit me, deep and hard into my neck, so that my life flashed before me and I feared the worst. After this he stood over me and laughed and said that, since I had seen what I should not have seen, I should have eyes no more. So he gouged my eyes out, Miss Whittle, then and there, and I screamed aloud for mercy but none did he show me, only taking to the sky on bony wings when I was sightless and quiet.

I woke up in the monastery, where you have stayed so lately, and Adam was by my side, having searched and found me when I did not appear later that day; he has aided me ever since. Yes, the bloodlust came over me and I was caged and chained, as is your fiancé, but Adam would not rest in his search for a cure…and, of course, you know the rest, Miss Whittle, you know the road he was prepared to travel for me. Have you got that devotion in your heart, I ask you? Are you ready to strike out on your own and free Frederick from an eternity of pain?"

He ceased speaking and took a long draught from the goblet he held.

"Thus concludes my story, Miss Whittle," he said, "And thus begins your own. On the morrow you must travel to take up the first challenge, if you decide to accept it. No-one can go with you, and beware those that do appear by your side to walk with you, for some are false prophets and seek only to divert you from your task and lead you astray. Helpers will be found on that lonely journey but they will flit into and out of your life on that path like summer butterflies that die when the first frost hits the land. In short, they are transient. Will you go, or will you return to those northern moors and forget Frederick, locked away from the world and only a stone's throw from the stake? Will you say to yourself, 'I will see him no more and thus evict him from my heart, and once that heart has healed I will love again and put all thoughts of Frederick behind me?' Which road will you choose, Miss Whittle? Which road?"

CHAPTER FOUR

They set out on the arduous journey home. Verity felt exhausted but in her hand she carried the old man's cudgel that he insisted she took with her.
"For, if you decline the road before you, there is still a long journey ahead until home is reached," he told her, handing over the stick with some pride, "Even though my eyes are no longer with me, the images of all that is beautiful around us stay in my mind and from them, I have been able to carve a tiger on the top. Rub him and he will protect you, wherever you are; on that long road to enlightenment or merely on the moors around your house. He has served me well and he will continue to do the same for you, I know. Remember my words...what I said earlier stands and although darkness shadows the road, good walks there too and it will find you if you are in danger."

Verity kissed him with some warmth as she knew that, but for him, she would indeed be going home, and without her beloved Frederick. Now, although she was leaving her betrothed behind, her journey was solely for him and about him.
"You mean to go then?" asked Adam, when they had negotiated the long climb down.

Verity was adamant.
"I do," she said and noticed that, although her heart beat faster, no doubts or negative feelings assailed her, "What you can do, Adam, so can I. Yes, I may seem like a weak and feeble woman but, I tell you, in here there beats a lion's heart."
"Maybe a tiger's would be more appropriate," replied Adam, making a grim attempt at humour, "Or should I say a tigress's?"

Verity fell silent as they approached the monastery. She knew the first challenge lay there, how to explain to Lawrence that she intended to go and find the things needed to release Frederick from his state of purgatory. Negotiate with a dragon, she thought with some trepidation. How did one do that?

Adam was speaking again and she asked him to repeat his question.

"I asked if you would like me to come with you and speak to Lawrence," he repeated, "After all, I have walked that road. I got to the end and my father stands whole and well before me."

Verity shook her head.

"I think I would like to tackle him alone," she said quietly, "Perhaps before nightfall and before Frederick becomes the monster he does when the sky is black and the moon shines."

"It would be as well," Adam acknowledged, "I have noticed his anger rising once the screams and the pleading start."

"How long shall I tell him I will be away, I wonder?" Verity said, more to herself than anything as they passed through the monastery gates, "And how shall I explain to him that I could not go home whilst there is a chance my beloved could be saved?"

"Sacrificing your life for his?" mused Adam, as they arrived at the refectory and sat down. Verity put her head in her hands.

"I thought you were on my side, Adam, and here to support me, not plague my mind with doubts," she said.

"I had many fears when I set out on my journey," Adam told her, "The night before I went I asked myself many times if this was possible and if dragons did grace our countryside and come out of the folklore mist to help us. However, when I saw the dark, liquid shine of his eyes as he sat in the palace and asked me why I troubled him I knew it was all worth it. Beware though, Miss Whittle, the false friends that may join you and declare they walk your way to keep you company. They seek to undermine your purpose and they will try to persuade you to give up your journey. You must focus on one thing only and that is to bring back the prize. Lawrence is not a young man and will not be able to cope with Frederick, as he is, for much longer. Speed is of the essence. You will struggle to walk as many miles as I did in a day but your rest must be brief and you must stop only when exhaustion has overcome you and your feet cannot take another step."

He fetched Verity some food and water, since she did not drink wine, and when that was consumed he said he must leave her and go to the chapel.

"I will pray for success for your journey," he told her, "You are in my heart and, as such, every time I pray, God will send you the strength you need to carry on. Remember to follow the map I have given you and beware demons disguised as good men. They will show their true colours soon enough but do not give them audience!"

"You had them in profusion then, I take it?" she asked, folding her napkin and wondering what she would do for food.

"Yes, the first week. However, by the second week, they could see the resolution in my stride and they left me alone. They are sent by the vampires of course, for you seek to reveal their secret and, in doing that, you then expose the means to destroy them. Whoever heard of bringing life to the Undead? All we could do before the secret was revealed was send them to heaven with a prayer for mercy. If that happens, Verity, and you fail, I will pray for Frederick's soul too. I cannot pray for his heart as that will still be locked up..."

"I shall unlock it!" declared Verity, jumping up, "I will bring it back with the witch and she shall restore it to him."

Adam nodded.

"Brave words," he acknowledged, "However, don't forget there is the dragon and he controls everything here, on this earth plane. He will only unlock Frederick's heart for the jewels you tempt him with, for his love of the bright and sparkling rules his whole being. The Palace of Reflections always needs another diamond, another emerald, another ruby! If you have the precious stones he will not refuse you but if you fail to acquire them….then he will be quite a different beast!"

"I have the notes you gave me," Verity told him, "Tonight I will sleep with them next to my heart and my soul will know every word of them when I set out on my journey tomorrow. Will I see you again before I go?"

Adam considered this.

"I am sure our paths will cross again," he murmured, "But if they do not, go with good grace and may God and all His angels be with you. I think you need luck tonight when you speak to Lawrence and try to convince him you have a chance to save the creature that causes him so much distress. He has talked many a time of using the stake and he will if Frederick gets out of hand. How can we stop him? True, in the eyes of the law it is murder but how can you murder someone who is already dead?"

On this rather pessimistic note he left her and the darkness grew in the long, echoing room. Verity made haste to tidy herself up and then to find Lawrence.

In the end she had to go full circle to find the man, as her journey down the long, dark stairs ended in a locked door where she could hear, dimly it is true, Frederick's moans from the cage behind the barrier. Her heart bled for him and if her resolve had weakened at all, his suffering, now clear in her mind, forced her on.

I am going on a journey for you, my dearest, her soul cried out. I may be some time, I do not know, but I have to try the only path open to save you.

And back came the perpetual cry from her beloved's soul "I am here...only feet away from you and if you come to me then we can share eternity together. Then my feet will follow your path and we will never be parted again. Come to me, Verity, come. Lawrence seeks to destroy me, I know and then the fires of hell could be my fate. Save me now! Do not set a foot outside this Holy Place! How the singing and the praising and the chanting burns my soul! We can be together...just one bite, just one and I promise you there will be no more pain…"

Verity jumped from her reverie and shook her head. She felt strong and determined.

I love you, Frederick, she sent back. I love you. Only enough to keep you away while I fight for you. I love you...

She could feel him drawing away from her and so she left the dim corridor and ascended to search once more. The monks were singing in the chapel and she paused for a moment to listen.

Would she ever hear them again, she wondered? And if she did manage to return would Frederick be dead and no longer Undead? There seemed no other path for him at the moment and, anxious to secure her interview, she left the chapel and went back to the refectory where she found the man she sought, eating his supper.

Her heart shuddered in revulsion as she saw the dead animal on his plate but she seated herself opposite him and bore his expression of surprise at the fact that she had not left.

"You duped me," he complained, gnawing the leg of lamb and letting the splashes of blood land on the table close to her elbows.

Verity hastily moved back.

"I shall speak to you when you have eaten," she replied, not wishing to stay near the odious smell of cooked flesh.

"What is there to say?" returned Lawrence, putting the revolting article down and wiping his hands, "You have disobeyed me and not left as you told me you would. There is no coach till Friday so I suppose we must put up with you until then. The Reverend Father will not be pleased. ONE night only, he told me, and then only if the woman sticks to the shadows and does not sit in our Holy places. Did you stray into the chapel, Miss Whittle?"

"No," she replied, "I lingered by the door and listened to the singing. Who could not pause when such wonderful voices are uplifted in prayer?"

"Ah...you ought to hear Frederick's voice uplifted in curses all night when I will not allow him to escape. I tie the chains pretty tight, Miss Whittle, but even so, he continues to beg and cajole. Were he to escape, your beauty would be sullied for sure!"

"I am aware of his sufferings, and yours too," she told him, sitting down again since he pushed his plate to the side, "And that is why I am going on a journey. To try to help."

"The best way for you to help is to head out of that door and never look back," Lawrence told her, "I was wrong to invite you here. Help yourself and go back to the life you had before Frederick knocked on your door."

Verity stood up to her full height and shook her head. "I am afraid I cannot," she told him firmly, "There is no going back. I have seen too much and I have heard too much. Tomorrow I shall leave here and go to try and bring Frederick's heart back. It will be a difficult and a dangerous path, I know but I have to try! I have talked to Adam and I have seen his father and now my plans are set in stone. All I ask from you is not to kill Frederick before I return."

Lawrence picked up a piece of bread and chewed on it, long and hard. Verity thought she had not been heard and repeated her words.

"Oh I know all about what Adam has been saying but he is a man, Miss Whittle, and you are a feeble woman. Besides, how do we know it is true? No one saw old Mr Curlious when he was a vampire, as his son locked him away and there are no monks here now that remember the incident."

"Adam would not lie!" flashed back Verity, continuing to stand in some defiance at his answer, "He has told me everything and I know now what I have to do. Yes, the path will be stony and steep in places but I have to try! How can I just go back and leave Frederick to his fate? You know you will have to kill him..."

"Killing the Undead eh..." interjected the man but Verity was not to be stopped.

"Don't split hairs with me, Lawrence," she almost shouted, "You will tire of him and he will get too powerful and then the only way IS the stake..."

"So you have another?"

"Yes," she replied confidently, "I do. I mean to follow in Adam's footsteps and retrieve Frederick's heart. Barter, lie, cheat, do anything to get it away from the dragon. It lies in a carved wooden box, Lawrence, where all the hearts of those that have been bitten lie and when they truly die, each heart returns to its body so that, intact, they ascend to heaven."
"Or they fall down, down, down into hell," put in Lawrence, "This is madness, Miss Whittle. You must tread a lonely road and there are demons guarding the dragon, demons who will take one look at you and convulse with laughter. It sounds more like a fairytale than fact and only Adam swears it is true. You could be making that journey for nothing and returning with nothing. You could lose your life. Go home, Miss Whittle, I say, go home!"
"I have no home now I have seen this," Verity answered, "Adam has told me of the Green Witch who will help me on the final stages of my path providing I bring her what she wants. Then, together, we can capture the jewels that will flash in the dragon's eye and lead to him opening the wooden casket to freedom!"
"Spare me the details, Miss Whittle, for I have heard it all when Adam is deep in the mead or the wine. I say I do not believe a word of it..."
"I have to believe," Verity told him, "I have to grasp at these thin shreds of hope. I cannot go home. Home for me has disintegrated into fragments and does not exist."

Lawrence was becoming very angry. He knew the hour was fast approaching when Frederick would require his full attention and now, this woman would not listen to his advice. He was tired and irritable and he banged his fist down on the table and forbade her to go.
"For God's sake, Miss Whittle, give up this insane scheme and go home!" he yelled, when she persisted in her plan.

Behind them, the door opened and a voice called, "Who is taking the name of our Lord God in vain? That I will not have in this Holy place!"

The man came forward into the candlelight and Verity saw his rich robes and the braid on his sleeve. Lawrence had the grace to look abashed.

"I am sorry, Reverend Father," he said, softly, "My mind was on other things and my heart was inflamed by passion."

Verity gazed at the man before her and bowed her head in reverence. She thought he turned to go so she called out after him,

"Sir, please do not leave yet! I am sure you know something of what we are arguing about and can aid me in my fight for justice! I am beholden to you for shelter here these past days..."

The man turned and looked at her for the first time.

"One night, Miss Whittle, I was assured it was, and yet I find you still here and causing raised voices in my monastery! Anger, Miss Whittle. Anger!"

"Righteous anger, sir! Righteous anger!" called out Verity as the man turned his back on her. He made as if to walk away and she ran after him and touched the sleeve of his robe, pleading with him to come back.

He turned to face her and she saw the compassion in his soul and reached out to it.

"Please sir, you know something of what I am going through! Lawrence does not believe what Adam Curlious says and he informs me there was no one here who saw the ritual that restored his father's heart to his body and drove out the vampire in him. So many people have had faith, sir, even though they have not seen Christ with their own eyes. Christ said he WAS love. I have faith, sir, that I can make this journey and restore my beloved to the upward paths. Please, if you know anything tell Lawrence now so that he may give me a chance to find that love and bring it home!"

The Reverend Father was moved by her words. He put out his hand and blessed her, trying to turn away and leave but truth barred the way.

"Was there no-one here who saw this?" she asked again, "For Lawrence says no-one apart from Adam can verify it is true. Please, sir!"

The man gave a great sigh and turned back to the two of them as expectant eyes met his gaze.
"I was here. I saw it," he admitted, "It is not a path I would choose to frequent but I saw it with my own eyes and I cannot deny it. Did not Peter deny the Lord and then bitterly regret it? I cannot live with regrets. I cannot walk out on a lie. I saw it and it happened."

CHAPTER FIVE

Morning came, red and warm, with the promise of heaven that spring mornings bring when the whole summer is ahead and winter is sleeping. Verity watched the scudding clouds part for the rising sun and she stroked the head of the cudgel she had been given and felt hopeful.

Her gratitude for the Reverend Father's words knew no bounds and she had left the two men to speak and retired to her room. She felt she had said enough and, besides, women were not countenanced at the monastery, and her presence there could be seen as inflammatory. Later, when the two men had conversed, Lawrence came to find her and she stepped out into the corridor to converse with him.

"Do I go with your blessing?" she asked him, her eyes searching his face for a grain of understanding.

Lawrence looked and felt awkward,

"I...I cannot go so far as to say you do," he replied, choosing to regard his feet rather than Verity's piercing eyes.

"But you understand a little more?" she suggested.

"Yes, and I believe the Reverend Father's words, although I still think it is foolish to run after a daydream."

"It is no daydream to me," she assured him, "Besides, what choice do I have? The one thin straw is offered as a slim chance of a route to freedom for both Frederick and myself, so I have to take it!"

"And if you fail?" he prompted.

She shrugged her shoulders.

"I will have done everything I could and at least I will have tried."

"But you could possibly perish in that attempt," Lawrence told her, "You asked me not to kill Frederick until you come back, but suppose you do not come back? Then what shall I do?"

"You must assume I am dead and put Frederick out of his misery."

"So how much time shall I give you? Suppose I kill the man just as you reach the monastery with your treasures?"
"The poem says that a black raven may do office as a messenger," Verity told him, "Where he or she comes from I do not know but I will try and get word to you."
"Not if you are dragon fodder," replied Lawrence pessimistically, "I cannot wait forever. Death will overcome me and then what will the monks do with Frederick?"

Verity nodded.
"I understand," she said, "You must do what you have to but please give me a few months!"

Lawrence looked worried.
"I will try," he told her, "However, there is only me and I have little help. Adam may watch the man during the day when he is quiet but, once he becomes active at night, it is all my responsibility. I risk my own life every night, Miss Whittle, merely struggling to contain Frederick."
"He is not Frederick then but a vampire seeking to strike," Verity told him, "I realise how hard it is for you but I have to undertake this journey. I have to try!"
"Your love must be strong," Lawrence admitted, "Time alone will prove if it is strong enough. I must go now, Miss Whittle. I wish you luck but I cannot say you go with my blessing."

Verity sighed. She realised she had built bridges but there was to be no perfect 'adieu'.
"Thank you for that," she said, "I wish you goodnight and a peaceful one too. Will I see you, before I leave at sunrise?"
"I think, or rather I hope, I will be sleeping by then," he told her, "However, my thoughts will be with you, and I pray for success in your travels," he bowed, gave her his hand and then was gone. She had listened to his footsteps fading into the darkness and then taken herself to bed. Strangely, after all the soul-searching, she had managed to sleep with no dreams to colour her rest and she had woken as the first bell sounded.

Six o'clock. Dawn. She stood over by the window and looked through the bars to the wide world outside. Soon she would be out there and alone, apart from her cudgel and her poem. Had Adam really followed its route to a safe conclusion? What if she fell at the first hurdle?

This, however, was not conducive to optimistic thought and she pushed it from her mind and began to get ready. She heard the monks singing sweetly in the chapel as she crept past and then, from the morning shadows, a tall figure approached her as she quit the monastery and walked out into the warm air.

"Brother Adam! You came to see me off!" she enthused.
"I could hardly let you go without at least one word of encouragement," he told her.
"So, have you any last minute advice for me?"

Adam sighed.

"Part of me wants you to turn around and go home," he told her, "However, in my heart, I know you are past listening and nothing I impart to you will stop your journey. And it was my journey not so long ago, and now my father stands, free from the parasitic infection that is vampirism. So how can I say anything but good luck and I will pray for you."

She smiled and gave him her hand,
"Until we meet again then," she said and drew off, leaving him standing there watching her go, his face impassive but his heart deeply troubled.

"My story now you won't believe,
Your heart is closed and so you grieve,
Your loved one lost and trapped in time,
So please pay heed now to my rhyme.
The steps you take, they number five,
So keep your hopes of help alive,
Come to the end and gather in
Five prizes that from death you'll win.
Snatch up the spoils, travel once more
And lay them at the dragon's door.
He has the very heart you seek,
So gird on pride, be strong, not weak.
When jewels a-plenty catch his eye,

He will not let your loved one die."

She knew the verse by heart, so many times had she read it since Adam thrust the faded document into her hand.

"Your first prize is the ouzel's tail,
A feather, black but also pale.
Where will he drop it…can you see?
Search in the woods, over the lea.
He sheds his plumage from the nest,
Gather it up, this is your test.
Remember, black but also white,
Half of him day and half in night."

An ouzel! She knew it was a bird but whether he was large or small and where he lived, she had no clue. Where did she go to search for him? North, south? She stood at the border of the monastery's land and stared back at the tree, now bursting into life. What was it saying to her? Could she listen, as the wind blew the greening branches this way and that? Was it just a plaintive melody or were there actually words in the rustle of its opening leaves? She listened for a moment more then, grasping her cudgel, she turned and headed north, away from habitation and away from the tormented face and soul of the man she loved.

She travelled on for some time, not really sure where she was going but following a path in her mind, at least. How would she find this elusive ouzel? A few times she stopped and peered into hedges but only small sparrows appeared, or she scanned the air and, though other birds flew over her head, they all had drab, brown plumage.
"An ouzel, an ouzel," she said aloud. Think back to your childhood, said her brain, what birds were in your picture books? Robins, wrens, chaffinches, crows…well, the latter were black enough but no white on them.

"A feather, black but also pale," she repeated. As if to answer her, a large, black crow soared overhead, taunting her it seemed, but not a vestige of white was on his feathers.

By midday she had reached a village and passed through its ancient streets. A few people stopped to stare at her but she ignored them and managed to buy a bread roll from a small shop near a church, as her hunger was sharp. Wandering into the graveyard to consume her simple meal, she found a jug of water, presumably kept there for flowers, and slaked her thirst.

Sitting on a seat by the church door, she finished her lunch and then picking a long piece of grass, she played with it idly, lost in thought. The opening of the church door made her jump and, when their eyes met, the tall, thin gentleman smiled and addressed her in a language she did not understand.

"I am not from around here," she told him, throwing away the spoiled piece of grass.

"You are English?"

"Yes."

She admired his Welsh lilt and his easy command of two languages.

"And what brings you to Aberroch?" he asked her when silence ensued.

She hesitated. Could she tell him the truth?

"I search for a black and white ouzel," she said at length.

His face registered surprise and she knew she had confused him.

"I am the incumbent of this parish," he told her, "If I can be of any help, please let me know."

She considered his offer in light of her quest.

"You possibly could be," she told him, "If you know of such a bird."

"What do you want from the ouzel?" he asked, "I have not heard that they make particularly good eating."

Verity was shocked.

"Oh, I wasn't wanting them for food at all!" she exclaimed, "It is a feather I need. However, not just any feather. I need a black and white one."

He looked puzzled at this and she expected him to ask for enlightenment but instead, he mentioned a woman in the village who, although retired now, was very knowledgeable about all species of birds.

"And do you think she will know what an ouzel is?" she asked him.

He smiled.

"Even I know what one of those is, although I spent a few years in London's smog," he said, "It is the country name for a blackbird."

The Reverend Sanderson was as good as his word and, although Verity felt very nervous of trusting a complete stranger, she sensed he was no time-waster.

"Beware false prophets and evil demons disguising themselves as good men to throw you off the trail!" Adam had warned her.

They left the churchyard and Sanderson offered her refreshment at his parsonage but she declined.

"I fear the flower water may not have tasted fragrant and my housekeeper makes very good tea," he assured her when she refused.

Verity shook her head. She was anxious to find out about ouzels and how she could obtain a feather, so tea drinking seemed a waste of time to her.

The Reverend accepted her refusal gracefully and said he would show her to the woman he believed could help her in her quest.

"And may I ask what it is for?" he ventured, "A bet? A sweetheart's dare?"

"You may ask," Verity told him truthfully, "but I am not at liberty to say. My lips must remain sealed for the moment, as there are demons about who are ready to push me off my path."

"Ah, yes," agreed the man of the cloth, "There are indeed, and my fight is with the ungodly and those that dabble in the Black Arts, against the scriptures I was brought up to believe in. I will just call into my home as we pass to get a weapon for you in your fight against the dark side of life."

They came to his door and he left Verity standing outside when she confirmed she would rather not step inside. She felt that, if she did, he would whisk her away for tea drinking and she would never escape. Sadly, there did not appear to be a Mrs Sanderson and she was surprised when he returned after a minute or two, and offered her a velvet box.
"Open it," he told her, pressing it into her hand.

She did as she was told and found a beautifully carved St Christopher, laying on an azure piece of velvet. Stunned, she turned questioning eyes to him. It was clearly a valuable piece and not one to bestow on a stranger.
"It was my sister's," he told her, "and therefore very precious but I knew, when I saw the pain in your eyes, that you need it to protect yourself on your travels. It served my sister for many, many years and kept her safe."

Verity was shocked that he would give it away and worried about what had become of his sister but he hurried on,
"Oh, her death was nothing to do with the beautiful necklace. She married a good man but died from complications while delivering her first child; complications which the old woman who served as midwife and the doctor we hired, could do nothing about. She told me to take the silver as she lay dying, telling me a time would come when I must give it to another who had a great need for it. I believe that time has come."

Verity was profuse in her gratitude and, putting it on, declared it made her feel safe at once.
"Although you have told me very little, I sense it is a precarious road you have to travel," he told her, pleased with her words, "and the way is littered with boulders and dead ends, which seek to trip you up and confuse you."

"Adam told me just that," admitted Verity, "He is a monk I know at Llanmorris Monastery and his father gave me this cudgel I carry."

"Then you are forearmed for the journey," the Reverend told her, taking her through a nearby cottage gate and rapping loudly on a cherry pink door.

The barrier was opened, after a minute or two, by an elderly lady dressed in rather tough tweeds and with a man's flat cap upon her head. Her style of attire did not seem to surprise Sanderson at all but Verity's eyes opened wider.

"Ah, Robin, I suppose you have found another waif and stray for me to help? Someone lost on their path who requires a little psychic intervention, eh?"

The Reverend frowned.

"Now, Rose, you know that is one area where you and I do not see eye to eye. I have come to bring this lady who seeks to consult you on your ornithological knowledge!"

"Why don't you just say birds, man? I apologise for Robin's turn of phrase, he has the dubious pleasure of being my nephew!"

Introductions were made and then Sanderson excused himself from Verity's far too pretty eyes and went back to write his sermon.

"The temptations of the flesh," he murmured as he left, "I am a priest first it is true, but I am a man also..."

Verity looked around the lofty hallway she had been invited into and felt suddenly cold.

"Take no notice of my nephew," his aunt assured her, "He means well but I know his words in English have a pompous stiffness and I presume you speak no Welsh?"

Verity admitted that she did not.

"So you are not from round here? A rough journey you must have had to reach the South West of Wales? And do you think we are all heathens here? Is that why you came to the church, where you must have met Robin?"

Confused by so many questions Verity shook her head immediately.

"I come from the Northern moors," she told Rose, "Previous to that, I lived close to London and, no, I do not view you as heathens at all. I sought the church for a drink, as I was thirsty, and for a quiet place to eat my lunch."

"So you are on a journey then, I believe?"

"I should more call it a quest," answered Verity, "A riddle...an enigma..."

"And, therefore, you may not get to the end?"

Verity sighed.

"I may not," she admitted, "Then my loved one will die and all my hopes of life go with him."

She was close to tears and Rose, who was a hospitable woman, told her to come into the parlour and rest. She offered a strange, green concoction which she called tea and Verity was comforted to find it smelt like the beverage that Adam had offered her at the monastery. She took a reviving sip and, feeling comforted, launched into her story.

Rose said not a word until Verity had finished and the girl was alarmed by this stilted silence.

"You do not believe me?" she ventured when a few more minutes had passed.

Rose shook her head.

"Oh no," she replied, "It is not that. I was just thinking who it was in the village who told me that a pied blackbird sometimes frequented her garden."

Verity's eyes widened.

"Really?" she said, "Really? I have a chance of solving the first riddle in the rhyme?"

Rose laughed.

"If we can get past Colonel Forster's mother and into her precious garden," she replied, "You may need to skulk in bushes and disguise yourself with branches, but it is not impossible. Finish your tea and we will go and throw ourselves on the Colonel's mercy. He proposed to me when Lionel died so I may have a tiny bit of influence over him, especially if we call once he has finished a large and luscious lunch. Gird up your loins and sally forth, child! Let Victory be ours for the taking!"

Verity was a bit confused by this but she did as she was told and the two set off to try and track down the elusive ouzel.

CHAPTER SIX

Verity shrank back at the impressive facade of the lofty hall in front of her but Rose, used to visiting the Colonel on various occasions for both business and personal reasons, told her companion that it was all show.
"The building has been neglected for years," she affirmed, "True, he keeps the cottage in good repair but only because his mother lives there and she still holds the apron strings. When she dies, I am sure he will pull the thatched place down and extend the park because the old lady will leave enough money to build this hall twice over!"

Verity shivered. There seemed a lot of sadness associated with the place and she did not like the heavy air of decay that seemed to permeate even the gardens that they now traversed.

Rose strode confidently forward but Verity tried to hide in the shadows of the shrubberies, feeling as if they were trespassing. Round the next corner they came across a tall, well-built man who had a strong military air and a handlebar moustache, twirled into a pattern that matched the clipped hedges bordering the property. Verity noticed the other hedges in the garden were straggly and overgrown.
"What are you doing here?" he barked, rather than shouted, "Keep off the lawns! They have just been seeded and a pretty penny they have cost too! Trespassers! No footpath here from the main road! Go back to the village!"

Rose drew nearer but Verity stopped in her tracks and wondered if they should have come unannounced.
"And nice it is to see you too, Colonel! Did you know it is five years to the day that you proposed to me and now you threaten me with all sorts of punishments for walking on what could have been my own land, had I said yes!"

The Colonel had the grace to look abashed at this and mentioned that he thought she was some travelling gypsy come from the village and seeking a shortcut across his land.

"In twelve guinea tweeds and with a fist full of rings worth a small fortune?" parried Rose, raising her heavily jewelled hands, "Why, if I was to give you just one of these diamonds you could get that dreadful park of yours done up so it was fit for royalty! Your eyes are no longer what they were to be honest, Bartholomew. However, we have not come to see you but your mother. Is she well?"

The Colonel gave a deep sigh.

"Sadly, she is," he affirmed, "And likely to be so for many more years according to the doctor. Why, she'll outlive me, for sure!"

"Complaining leaves a sour taste in my mouth," Rose told him, "We have been friends for long enough to know you will not do a thing about it. She controls you as much now as she did when you were a babe-in-arms!"

"True, true," grumbled the Colonel, "So, who have you brought with you, skulking in the shrubberies as though I am the devil incarnate?"

Rose laughed and told Verity to come forward.

"He is a miserable old man," she told her new friend, "However, I trust his judgement and underneath this stiff, starchy exterior there beats a kind heart. This lady is on a quest that your mother may be able to help us with, Bartholomew."

The Colonel raised his eyes to heaven.

"Good luck in getting an audience with her," he told the two women, "She is having her afternoon rest and I dare not disturb her until 4 o'clock, when she will expect her maid to provide a cup of the finest tea. Oh how she will cuss if it is not brewed long enough! Three girls come and gone in less than a year! Come and look at my spring flowers whilst the old hag sleeps and tell me more of your quest, Miss…?"

"Whittle," replied Verity, deciding to use her real name.

"Ah, Miss Whittle, and what brings you to the wilds of West Wales? Not its beauty surely?"

"No, sir, for I had never heard of the place until recently. I am come to find a pied ouzel and Mrs…er…"

"Rose," put in the aforementioned lady.

"Yes, and Rose said you may have one here?"
"God knows! God knows! My mother delights in feeding the birds so she would know," replied the man, offering Rose his arm for a tour of the gardens. "Ladies, come with me and while away a pleasant hour by wandering along my fragrant paths, if you please!"

Rose seemed easy in the Colonel's company but Verity felt the place was depressing and overgrown and she was longing to see the ouzel and put her mind at rest. However, she realised time had to pass before she could consult the Colonel's mother and she was glad of any diversion so that the nature of her quest was secret a little longer. It had been bad enough to have to reveal so much to Rose, who she barely knew.

Most of the paths were so overgrown with weeds and grass, even this early in the year, as to be impassable but the Colonel produced an old-fashioned scythe that he declared his mother had swung in her heyday and cut the offending vegetation down.

"She would be out here now, organising the gardeners and shouting at me, had not a bout of rheumatism laid her low," he affirmed.

"Since when did you have a gardener...or at least one that you paid," Rose asked him, with direct bluntness.

"Hmm," replied the Colonel, "Wouldn't hurt you to put in a few hours and melt away some of that fat of good living that has accumulated over the past years!"

Rose laughed long and hard.

"What a flatterer you are, Bartholomew!" she replied, "Come, I think we have wandered far enough. We shall come to the borders of your land where Welsh dragons brood and have their lairs, so overgrown are those woods!"

"My mother says the birds love the land that way and will release no money to have it cleared and planted with crops as I suggested. Let Mother have her tea first as she will be in a better mood; and come into the orangery, where I am attempting to grow exotic fruits!"

"With no success," whispered Rose to Verity, who followed close behind her, "For five years he has spent a small fortune on trying to produce a pineapple and all he has got is a shoot that withers and dies."

Bartholomew heard most of that and agreed he possessed not one green finger. They entered the orangery and the Colonel produced chairs for the ladies; as the day was warm he opened a few windows. He rang a bell a few times and a smartly dressed lady appeared with whom he put in an order for tea.

"So that is the latest one," murmured Rose, as Verity stared around her but remained silent, "How long will she stay, Bartholomew, when she finds out your mother will only pay half of what you have promised?"

The man scowled.

"Have you come here just to make fun of me, woman?" he asked the unrepentant Rose.

"Ah, it could have been worse, for I could have said yes to your proposal and then I could've teased you night and day without ceasing, as would be my right as a wife. I have not set foot in the place for a good fortnight so you have had comparative peace!"

"Peace?" cried the Colonel, "I have not had a vestige of peace since Mother took up refuge in my cottage..."

"HER cottage," replied Rose, smiling.

The tea was brought and served but Verity struggled to swallow a drop and refused the small, hard cakes. Her mind immediately went back to Liddy's cakes and she wondered if she would ever taste them again. A tear fell into her cup but she remained silent.

"The cakes are like rocks, Bartholomew, so maybe this one is not marriage material," Rose acknowledged, "Or have you already asked her? Best to test her baking first, I believe."

"Hmm...they seem calculated to break every tooth I have in my head," replied the Colonel, "Best soaked in the tea but even then hardly edible."

Rose tittered in delight.

"Yet you enjoyed the sponge I made you when we first met," she confirmed, "You ate every crumb and licked your fingers free from icing I seem to remember."
"After that delight I got down on one knee and did the deed!" the Colonel pondered.

Rose laughed all the harder.
"That you did not," she told him, "You were suffering from an attack of gout and could barely walk across the room to address me!"

Bartholomew shrugged and dunked a sizeable chunk of cake in his tea but he could only gnaw at it and he affirmed it was only fit for the pigs.
"She will have to go," he said sadly, "Mother, however, will take great delight in that, especially when she tries to eat the cake that is served to her today. Having no teeth she may resort to sucking it but the flavour is not one I would cherish."
"Indeed, no," replied Rose, leaving her cake uneaten on the side of her saucer and noticing that Verity had avoided the cakes completely.

At length, the Colonel conceded that his mother would have woken, supped and complained to her heart's content and the two ladies could risk a visit.
"Will you come and announce us?" Rose asked her former beau but he shook his head and backed off.
"Connection forces me to be so often in her company that I shall leave this to your silver tongue, Rose," he told her, "Besides which, if I attend, I shall never hear the last about the cakes. I shall be forced to listen to her yards of complaints at dinner, so please, give me a few hours of peace, at least!"

Rose laughed heartlessly at this and the two ladies rose and made their way out. The Colonel followed and took Rose's hand and kissed it.
"Goodbye then, dear lady, I leave you to your fate!"

He bestowed a similar goodbye to Verity and then drew off.

"Coward!" shouted Rose, waving at him but he pretended not to hear and very soon he was out of sight.

Rounding the corner of the dark and overgrown shrubbery the two women made their way to a gate in the corner of the lawn and, going through it, found themselves in a small garden with a gravel path winding to the door of a thatched cottage.

"Let us hope that dear Madeline did not have the inedible cakes that we did," Rose prayed.

"They looked and sounded like boulders," Verity admitted, feeling she needed to break her pensive silence and speak.

Rose knocked at the well polished wooden door and a girl opened it with a curtsey and asked for the visitors' names.

"Mine will mean nothing to her," Verity whispered.

Rose nodded and proceeded to give her own.

"Tell her Mrs Stebbings is here to see her, please," she told the girl, who then bade them enter and ushered them into a small drawing room.

She was not absent long and came back in with a smile, saying that Mrs Whitworth would be pleased to see them both. Verity followed Rose and they both ascended the rather creaky stairs to be announced.

"Mrs Stebbings and one other."

Verity hung back, rather worried about this fierce woman, but Rose strode ahead, kissed Madeline's much-wrinkled hand and asked her how she was.

The old lady sat in an upholstered armchair with a rug over her knees, although the day was warm, and her quick, little bird-like eyes darted everywhere. She was small to the point of slight but mentally alert and she spotted Verity's hesitancy at once.

"Mrs Stebbings, how pleasant to see you again. I trust you are not here to tell me you are going to be my daughter-in-law in the future?"

Rose laughed.

"No, no," she told Madeline, "There is no fear of that, so do not worry. I have come to introduce a friend of mine who has a particular interest in that pied ouzel you have in your garden."

Madeline's gimlet eyes darted onto Verity who was unsure what to do, so she curtseyed and remarked it was nice to meet her ladyship.

"Ha ha, now that is a good one," replied the old lady, "You have given your friend lessons in flattery I see. Come forward child, and tell me what you want with my pied ouzel."

Verity did as she was told and remarked that all she needed was a feather.

"I see," remarked Madeline, "So what is the feather for, may I ask? A private collection...although they usually want eggs. He is a fine and bonny bird and I do not want to lose him."

"Oh no," replied Verity, horrified that she was seen as a danger to the bird. "I would wait for him to lose one and not try to pluck it from him. I mean the bird no harm."

"It intrigues me what you want it for," grumbled Madeline, "I can ask the girl to search the garden yet again for a feather but I fear nothing will be found."

"You have already looked, then?" queried Rose who had sat down, unasked, on the edge of the old lady's bed. She wriggled her toes in the over tight boots.

"Of course! As how else could I prove I had a rare species in my garden? I thought to show you, Mrs Stebbings, since you seem to be the local authority on birds in this area."

"And very interested I would have been too, but it seems my friend's need is greater as she requires one for a teaching project she is undertaking. Maybe we could look for ourselves and save the maid a job?"

"A teacher, eh?" replied Madeline, missing nothing, "What do you teach the young savages then? Manners would be the best thing, not about birds' feathers. The hoodlums have come once from the village to my garden to try and rob my nests of eggs. Old Benson, my dog, saw them off. Are they your lot?"

Verity remarked, in all truthfulness, that she did not teach in this village.

"Ah...then I see you are not responsible and it did not matter that Benson got one of them and tore the seat of his pants," replied the old lady, "Yes, Mrs Stebbings, look to your heart's content and if you do find one please let me see it before the school boys are allowed to."

Rose got off the bed and smoothed the coverlet down. "Thank you very much," she said, with a polite bow, "I trust if we do not find one we may come back and look again?"

Madeline waved her hand.

"Of course, of course," she acknowledged, "As many times as you wish. All I ask is that I see the feather before it leaves the village!"

Verity stood in the garden unsure of what to do.
"Should I wait in the bushes?" she asked Rose who, she felt, knew more about elusive birds than she did, "Will he or she come down to feed if I am here?"

Rose considered the question.
"It is very unlikely," she admitted, "Of course, I have never seen a pied ouzel and I wonder if the old lady's eyes have played tricks on her. Or of course the wine she likes to imbibe may have done that," she added.

"Is there anyone else here who would know?" asked Verity, worried her precious time was being wasted and this particular avenue was, in fact, a dead end.

"Well, she used to have a gardener, though heavens only knows how he stayed when she paid him so little. The place looks quite overgrown but we could have a look around to see if he still exists. Maybe she has a boy coming from the village who she pays a farthing to."

No sooner had she said these words than a gaitered individual bore down upon them and told them they were trespassing.

"Oh, not again," replied Rose in despair.

"No right of way through here!" shouted the elderly man, waving his arms about and dropping a quantity of vegetation he had obviously been cutting, on to the grass. Verity, trying

to be helpful, picked a few handfuls up for him but he shouted at her to lay off and was bristling with anger.
"The right of way was boarded up years ago!" he continued, "I'll have the authorities onto you, making free with Madam's garden for your perambulations!"

Verity would have gone but Rose was made of sterner stuff and besides, she believed she had an open invitation to the place any time she chose.

Stepping forward she snapped her fingers to get the man's attention and said in a cool, calm voice,
"Excuse me but I could ask whether YOU were actually the trespasser! I am Mrs Stebbings, an old friend of both Madam, as you refer to her, and to the Colonel, so much so that we are on first name terms. We have seen your 'Madam' and she has given us carte blanche to frequent her garden as much as we like in order to seek out an ouzel's feather!"
"A likely story," was the reply, whilst even more vegetation escaped his angry arms, "If you will wait here I shall check with Madam as to the validity of it. I have never seen you before and have been gardener here for three months now."
"Do as you wish," Rose told him, "But we have come to seek the pied ouzel that the Colonel told me about. Have you seen the bird too or is it a figment of imagination when a drop too much is taken?"

The man was about to depart but, at the mention of the bird, he turned back and murmured he had seen the confounded thing.
"It isn't a 'thing', it is a 'he' or 'she'," Verity reminded him.

He took a long, hard look at her, as she had not spoken before, and mentioned that all birds and animals were 'its'.
"Maybe to YOU," replied Verity, "But I happen to think differently. ALL creatures have as much personality and character as we do. Why..."

Rose cut her short.
"Have you seen the bird?" she asked.
"Yes, and taken many a pot-shot at it too but always missed sadly."

Verity was angry.

"Does Madam know you are doing this?" she retorted, "If not, I shall march in and tell her!"
"Abominable women!" replied the man "Always interfering! What do you want the bird for anyway? It's too thin to make a decent meal and there are barely enough feathers for a hat!"
"We don't want to harm the bird in any way!" shouted Verity, thoroughly angry. "We just want ONE pied feather, that is all. Have you seen one?"

The man shook his head.
"That I haven't," he replied, "I don't want no feathers making a mess in this garden. There is enough to do. Now I must check with Madam," and dropping the rest of the greenery on the ground he walked off.

Rose raised her eyebrows and Verity shook her head. The pied ouzel seemed as elusive as ever.

It was two hours later and, concealed in the hedges, neither Verity nor Rose had had as much as a glimpse of a bird. It was hot now and Verity removed her cloak and laid it across the trunk of a fallen tree at the edge of the grass.

The gardener had returned in a better frame of mind, having been told by Madeline that the two ladies were permitted to remain until the bird was sighted and, furthermore, they would be allowed to come back and search for a feather in the days that followed. Gareth was not pleased but, as his job was fairly easy and time was his own, he was forced to bite his tongue and be civil to the ladies at least. Having to bring them refreshment galled but he left the glasses on the base of a tree and got on with his work.

Rose went to fetch the water and murmured that she would have to go home in a minute as she had chores to do and besides her stomach was rumbling.
"Those so-called rock cakes were hardly a substitute for my afternoon tea," she complained, "You must stay with me tonight, Verity, for I sense this could be a long job and many are the days your eyes will be glued to the skies, hedgerows and trees for the prize you desire."

"I cannot move on without the feather," replied Verity, wondering how Adam managed to obtain such an article. "The verses must be dealt with in strict order and one task completed before setting off on the next. I worry the bird has been shot or killed by this man we saw. Perhaps he wounded him or her and our only find will be a corpse or even worse a skeleton."

"You could at least get a feather that way," replied Rose, ever practical.

"It would be no prize, no victory, for it to come off a body," Verity told her, "I am trying to save life, not end it. I have to approach these tasks with compassion in my heart. A dead bird is a hollow victory and I would move on to my next riddle with doubt and fear. No good can come of murdering living beings for a token."

At length Rose said she must go but that she would come back in an hour or so and sit with Verity until dusk descended.

"You must eat, too," she told the girl, "Nothing was ever achieved on an empty stomach and the spirits fall and deflate when hunger sets in."

"I am not hungry," replied Verity, keeping her eyes peeled, "My inner senses are numbed whilst I search for what will bring me the heart of my beloved. I would go without food and water for days could I bring him back into my life. I have this one chance and I must not waste it."

Rose bade her goodbye and left the canopy of trees. Now Verity was alone and the gardener crept up on her to remove the glasses and remind her that he was going home in less than an hour.

"So the garden will be locked up," he said, "and I do not think Madam will want to be disturbed once her dinner is served. I will come and warn you once I have finished trimming the far side of the shrubbery. If you see the bird I could trap him tomorrow and then you can pluck him or I can try my gun again."

Verity was very angry.

"There will be no bloodshed here," she said.

"But it is much quicker than waiting for him to drop a feather!" cried Gareth, getting vexed. "How long will that take? Better to kill the thing and then pluck off what feather you require."

"I tell you that no trapping or murdering innocent creatures will take place!" shouted Verity, furious now with his cruel attitude, "I will wait for however long it takes for him to shed a feather painlessly. I will search every inch of this garden for one and if that takes weeks then so be it!"

Gareth went off, his moustache bristling with anger and left her to it. The sun was just beginning to wane as the afternoon wore on and Verity closed her eyes against its heat and power. Did she sleep? Did she dream?

On the lowest bough of a nearby tree, just out of reach of the hedgerow where she rested a bird alighted. She blinked her tired eyes against the glare of the spring sunshine and saw that he was a medium size and that his feathers were of a black and white hue. She smiled in delight and put out her hand to him.

The bird shook his pied feathers and told her,
"You could have had me trapped, killed for one feather but your kind and compassionate heart chose not to. You could have trodden the easy path and murdered me, pulling the feathers from my feeble body and picking the very best to take on your journey but you were prepared to wait. How hard it is for my precious brothers and sisters in this world of humans! Mankind just do not see that we have feelings too."
"But I do!" cried Verity, "I can see you are just like me and you feel pain, anger, hope and joy. Why should I take away your life for one feather? What right have I to do that? I will wait and wait for you to shed one in your own time and I will protect you from any who seek to harm you whilst I am here!"

The bird whistled a merry tune.
"There is no need for you to wait," he told her, "You have proved, by your words and actions, that you deserve a feather and, besides, speed is the watchword on your

journey. Come with me now and I will show you where I moulted out a fine tail feather this morning! Follow me!"

Verity found herself running after the bird whilst he flew a few feet ahead and at the end of the garden he landed on a tree trunk and pointed with his wing to where a fine feather lay amidst some rotting leaves left over from the autumn trees.

"There!" he said, "Take it with pleasure and go on your way! For your compassion I bless you and I must do one thing for you before I return to my life. What task shall I perform for you? If it is within my power, I will do it!"

Verity picked the feather up and pressed it to her heart. "A letter!" she said, "A letter! I could write a letter to Adam to tell him I have the first prize and please, please to make sure my beloved stays Undead whilst I search for the other treasures. Would you do that? Could you do that with your wonderful pied wings? Carry the letter to the monastery and drop it at Adam's feet as he wanders in the grounds and wonders if I am alive or dead..."

The ouzel clapped his wings together and vowed he would call for the letter tonight.

"I know where you rest your head tonight," he said, "It is not so far from here and I will come a little before midnight and collect the letter. Then I shall fly to the monastery and perform my task! Once I have done that my magical powers will leave me and I shall be an ouzel once more."

"Stay safe and I will see you later," replied Verity, returning to pick up her cloak and waving to the bird as he flew off.

A magical ouzel, she thought. My compassion gave him that voice and won me my first prize.

Exhausted and triumphant, she returned along the lane to Rose's cottage, her heart hopeful that she would succeed in winning her next prize, whatever that was to be. The sun slid down the sky and the evening shadows came in with a chill breeze but Verity was lost in a daydream which brought her beloved Frederick to her side and banished the bitter gall that entrapped his soul.

CHAPTER SEVEN

"My Dearest Lawrence and Brother Adam,
Success has been mine regarding the first prize and I hold in my hand the rare and precious pied ouzel's feather, which will surely delight the witch when I present it to her later this year. Lawrence, I know you do not believe in such things, you having come to the monastery after Adam achieved the five prizes to barter for his father's heart, but believe me when I say these things exist and are facts.

I remain in hopeful spirits after the ouzel bird recognised my compassion and showed me the very place where he had shed a feather a few hours earlier. Hidden in a dusky dell I would never have stumbled across it and would very likely be waiting there now, under the hedges, for another feather to fall. Thus am I now relieved of the first of my tasks; it is accomplished, and the very bird to whom I showed compassion is set to transport this letter to you before he returns to what he is in reality, a Welsh ouzel bird."

Verity sat back from her letter writing for a moment and luxuriated in the comfort of the rug beneath her and the warm cup of tea that stood on the dresser. She looked at the bed that was hers for the night and knew that this was a picture unlikely to be repeated in her quests for the remaining four prizes. She bent again to her letter.

"Tell Frederick I love him and miss him, but not too much or too often of course, and although you may not hear from me for a while until my other four prizes are collected and exchanged, believe me always,
Your loving
Verity. "

She put down her pen and heard the clock downstairs strike the hour. Midnight. Was that a flutter of wings at the window, she wondered?

She rose and pulled up the blind and saw the outline of the ouzel bird on the sill. He had come. He had kept his word. Shaking free the window she called to him and he turned to view her with his bright eye.
"Ouzel bird! Ouzel bird!"
"I am here!" was his muted reply.
She took a minute or two to stroke his feathers and caress his head and then she brought forth the letter and he took it in his bill. With a wink of his black orb he flew from the house and up, up, up into the night sky and she saw him no more but she knew, in her heart, he would achieve his goal.

"Please Adam, if you can, make a spot of safety and calm for this ouzel bird in the monastery garden, so that when I return from my mission I may see him and know he is protected. For, as with every living thing, he is unique and precious beyond all measure."

She closed the window and went downstairs where Rose was still up, turning over the pages of some old ornithology guide and making notes.
Verity placed her empty cup and saucer in the kitchen and told her host she would now go to bed.
"So, will you move on in the morning, since you have achieved your goal here?" asked Rose, suddenly loath to lose her guest. It was very rare anyone actually stayed with her.
"I shall," replied Verity, "I shall leave with a heart full of gratitude for your help and with the ouzel feather tucked into my bag as I take the first step on the rest of my long, hard journey. Will the other prizes be as easy to win, I wonder? Time will tell but of one thing I am sure, I will never find such an exquisite place to lay my head and tomorrow night, I wonder, where will I be?"
Rose smiled.
"I have enjoyed helping you," she acknowledged, "My prayers will go with you and I hope the road is not paved with boulders to trip you up! Beware who you meet on that road! There are many evil people out there and your quest is

lonely for no-one can go with you! Have you read the next verse which guides your footsteps on the morrow?"
"I have," replied Verity, "It is written on my heart now and will fill my ears as I sleep. I head for the Welsh coast and would be grateful on the morrow if you can point out the path I must take to get there. The sky was red and orange when I looked out about 8 o'clock tonight so the coming day promises fair."

Rose said she would fill Verity's bag with food and drink in the morning and make her breakfast before her feet trod the road to the sea.
"For now then, goodnight," she told her guest and Verity turned from the night and sought the transient refuge of sleep.

"My second prize in water deep
Where salty fishes come to sleep;
And hid inside a coloured shell,
A rarity the Welsh know well,
A snail found only on this shore
His small pink home will be the door,
The window to your loved one's heart
So get your bearings and depart
To where the great orme rears his head
The worm of Wales, who has been said
To bring his chargers to the sand
And send a storm to rule the land
Take you this prize – then on to three
Beware the tides….as you will see."

It was morning and as fine a morning as late May could muster, with the dew drying on the grass and hedges and small birds carolling their love of the spring when they could bring forth their young. The mist turned the lane into a mysterious land but the sun rose and burnt off the haze, and drew fanciful patterns on the lawns of the small village.

Verity watched the progress of the day from her bedroom window. How calm and peaceful everything looked! A small part of her wanted to remain here, never moving, never thinking, but the silence was broken by the shout for breakfast. Verity smiled. Rose had a large voice and an even larger heart.

Once she had eaten and her bag was packed, Verity walked with Rose in the cool of the early morning and found the path that undulated down to the sea. Rose turned to face her guest and there were tears in her eyes.

"Will I see you again?" she asked in a voice quite unlike her usual one.

"I think it is likely," replied Verity, "I may have to come back this way when the rest of my prizes are won, and a warm bed and a kind heart would really help to lessen the loneliness of my travels."

"You are bound to meet people far more interesting than me," Rose told her but Verity shook her head.

"I must beware of false prophets Brother Adam told me," she mused, "I do not expect to come across one with such a large heart as you!"

Rose was pleased and they parted by the narrow path which, Rose assured her friend, would broaden out to a wide thoroughfare soon enough.

"For it bypasses the village and then meanders out to the estuary and from there on to the coast," she told her friend.

Standing waving her handkerchief till Verity was out of sight, Rose felt a sudden pang of anguish that her friend could be in danger but she dismissed it and sent blessings tumbling after the walker.

"Protect her and guide her God," she whispered and then turned her face to her cottage and home once more.

Verity walked for a full hour and then, wiping her head of perspiration, for the day was growing warm, she espied up ahead a soldier who was walking with military precision, his army backpack swinging gently on his shoulder. She tried not to catch up with him but, even though she thought she had slowed her pace, his form became nearer and nearer and she was obliged to stop and let him get further ahead as she desired no company on her walk to the Welsh coast.

As Rose had said, the path began to widen out and to meander as it made its journey to the sea and many was the corner Verity rounded expecting to see the soldier in the distance but his form was not visible, so she concluded he must have stepped off the path, for whatever reason.

Turning an even sharper bend she was confused to find him sitting on a stone singing to himself as he drank from a bottle and carved off slices of meat from a small joint he had obviously taken from his backpack. He smiled at Verity and offered her a slice but as it was what the woman regarded as dead, tortured flesh she turned her head away and refused.
"I saw a maid all dressed in blue
And like a summer sky;
The rainbows fell from her sweet lips
As she went roving by," he sang with an eye on Verity as she pushed on and passed him.
"So where are you going, my sweet maid?" he called to her as she overtook him.

Verity chose not to answer him and quickened her pace but he packed up his belongings and followed her, singing loudly so as to attract her attention:
"As I was a-walking one morning in May,
I spied a young couple a-making of hay;
The first was a young girl and her beauty shone clear
And the second was a soldier, a bold grenadier..."
With half an ear on his song, which was tuneful and mellow despite the volume, Verity carried on her journey and had to admit he had a good voice. However, after another few verses there came one that was not to her liking and, believing he had deliberately sung it to embarrass her, she stopped and swung round.
"At his words then this young girl she sank to the ground,
And the hay was all scattered, all scattered around.
"If you go back and leave me for your sweet wife so mild
In autumn's chill breezes I will bear you a child."

Their eyes met and the young man smiled but Verity was clearly vexed.

"Stop your song!" she almost shouted at him, "For I'll hear no more of it and the sentiments it contains! Why it is positively bawdy and not one for the ears of ladies! You may yell it in the pubs you doubtlessly frequent with the undesirable company you surely keep but I seek peace and quiet on my walk! This is a beautiful place do you not think and yet you are ruining it for all who walk this way!"

The young man essayed a bow and remarked he saw no other beings but herself on the path at this moment.

"I do see beauty though, as you said," he continued, "Rare and precious beauty and much in the scenery that is to my liking!"

Verity was even more vexed as she knew that he alluded to her person. She pulled her scarf a little tighter around her neck and told him to leave her alone.

"Since we both chose to walk this path at the same time, I am afraid I cannot do that," he admitted.

"Then rest where you are and let me go ahead," she told him.

"Or we could make a bright day even brighter by travelling together," he suggested, "You are going to the coast and so am I. Why don't we swap stories as we travel the next four miles?"

Verity looked at him and saw much to like but her suspicions were up and she declined his offer.

"I will be the one to wait then," she told him, "Since you seem to be in such a hurry. I will sit here on this rock in the sun and wait for you to get out of sight before I start walking again."

The young man shook his head.

"That is very sad," he said, "Do you not feel a stirring of curiosity for my story?"

"No," came the firm reply.

"And yet, I feel a strong interest in my fellow traveller. The day is still young and I could spare an hour listening to you if you want to remain here and talk."

"You remain and I will go on then," replied Verity, standing up, "You seem to be determined to be as cussed as you can!"

The young man laughed and told her he meant no harm. "I usually miss out the next to last verse of that song when ladies are present," he admitted, "I sang it to see whether it would provoke you into entering into some sort of conversation with me and it has done that."
"Very unwillingly, I assure you," from Verity, "Now, I desire that you walk on and leave me please."

The young man bowed low.
"Very well," he said, "I will bother you no more."

He was as good as his word but she heard the last verse of the song floating back on the breeze to her ears as he rounded the next bend.
"And he kissed her and he left her and she watched him go by,
But a tear trickled down from his hazel brown eye:
Yes, he ran to his wife and his children's whim,
One wife and the army was plenty for him!"

Verity waited a while, until she felt there was a safe distance between her and the annoying young man and then she shouldered her bag, took up her staff, and started off once more. An hour went by and she never saw another soul but the salty tang of the sea began to accompany her and she sniffed long and hard at the air. She had only seen the mighty ocean once, when she was a child and her parents had taken her to a northern beach with miles of golden sands. Memories came back to her, sharp and poignant, and she wiped away a tear and quickened her pace.

The way became far more rocky and she had to climb over a few boulders that blocked the path whilst the screams of seabirds rent the air.
"Another mile or so and I am there," she said, out loud, to boost her courage.

Now the track plunged dramatically downhill and a strong breeze eddied around her so she pulled her cloak on and felt suddenly chilled. Dark, ominous clouds gathered overhead but she pushed on, only stopping for a drink of water from the bottle Rose had given her that morning. Hunger had deserted her entirely after the encounter with the young man. "I bet he was a demon, sent to tempt me from my path and confuse me," she said aloud to justify her harsh words to him, "God knows where I would be if I had stopped to listen to his story. Then there was his song..." and she shuddered at the memory.

The path climbed once more and she found herself seriously out of breath. A pain in her side forced her to stop and she panted. For a moment the scenery blurred and darkened. Nibbling on a square of Rose's bread for nourishment gave her tired body fuel and she felt less weak so that, blown and anxious, she eventually stood at the stormy summit.

Sure enough, down below, the sea shone deep and cold as a few rays of sun crept through the clouds and illuminated the view. It looked as though the tide was coming in judging by the way the grey sands were being covered by the dancing white chargers the water sent. Verity was mesmerised by it.

To think, down there, somewhere, was the rare Welsh snail she needed to save her beloved.

The path down to the beach was even more treacherous and she slipped several times, keeping her balance by holding on to the larger rocks that strewed the steep track. Suddenly she felt herself falling into space and she closed her eyes, expecting to be dashed to pieces on the sharp rocks but, no sooner had she begun her fall than she was conscious that a strong arm grabbed her and stopped her journey. She opened her eyes to see a tall figure standing over her, holding onto her waist and pulling her bag away from the edge of the precipice.

"Steady! Steady!" he told her, putting her bag beside her, "You may have hit your head. Do you feel sick?"

She shook her head and turned to look at him. For a moment she thought it was the young man who had gone ahead but she realised this man was older and fair of skin and face.

"You took a proper tumble then," he told her, as she climbed to her feet and smoothed down her dress and cloak.

"Where did you come from?" Verity asked him, "I saw no-one on the footpath and you must have run down here to catch me up."

"I saw you down below me a while ago," said the man, handing her the bag, "I walk fast as I know this coast like the back of my hand having fished the waters man and boy."

"So you are a sailor then?" replied Verity, excitedly.

"Yes."

"And you know these waters, so you can help me in my quest to capture the rare pink periwinkle snail?"

"Ah...yes and I even know the rocks where a few of them are left after the Welsh have picked them for their puddings!"

"Puddings?"

"Yes, sea salt pudding and very nice it was too, as I remember."

"Yuk...you have eaten these snails?"

"Not recently but as a boy, certainly. Would you like me to show you the rocks where they reside?"

Verity threw all caution to the wind and mentioned she would like that very much.

Here was the second prize, all wrapped up and hers for a song...having Frederick back in her arms seemed suddenly close and real.

CHAPTER EIGHT

Verity and her new companion made their way slowly down the rest of the steep slope and arrived, tired and breathless, at the bottom. The tide was clearly on the way in and visible rocks, where Verity had planned to search for the elusive snail, were fast becoming covered with swirling water.

The sailor, who said his name was Daniel, opened the bag he carried on his back and offered Verity some fruit, which she gladly accepted. Her guard was down and the second prize seemed to be offered to her on a plate, so she took the apples and fine red tomatoes he held out and relaxed on a large stone by the entrance to a small cave.

"How long will the tide take to turn?" she asked her new friend, who replied it would be a couple of hours, at least. He too, seemed very relaxed although she noticed he did not eat or drink but watched her as though he was concerned for her welfare.

"You took quite a fall up there," he told her, "You were so close to the edge and, had I not come along, you could have been pieces on this beach for the tide to take out."

"Heaven forbid!" cried Verity, "I am extremely lucky to have had your help but now I release you from that bond and am quite happy to wait here by myself until the tide goes out and I can search those rocks and streams for my prize!"

The man smiled and mentioned it was no trouble to wait with her until the water subsided.

"At high tide these rocks are covered so we will have to move further up the beach but we are safe for the next hour I am sure."

"You must know this area very well if you have been a sailor," Verity said when the conversation lulled.

"My family were sailors and my brother still fishes the seas about here," Daniel told her, "The sea is in my blood and, I swear, I know every boulder and pebble on this beach, for I have walked over here since I was a small boy. The water may be cold but would you not like to refresh your feet in the healing salt water if you have walked far?"

Verity considered and told him she would like that very much and they approached the incoming tide and the swirling grey-green water. Verity felt a fleeting sensation of fear but she let it wash over her, like the sea water, and found pleasure in the coolness refreshing her toes. Daniel was some distance ahead of her and she watched him walking confidently through the deepening water until he stopped, gazed down and called out to her,
"Come and look at this!"

Verity waded out to where he stood, conscious that the water was now up to her thighs and wetting her dress and cloak. She barely had time to ask him what it was when he turned to her and his eyes flashed red in the weird grey light. She screamed and tried to turn away but he was on to her in an instant and she felt him pushing her down so her face was in the water and her lungs were filling with it…
"No, No," she cried, but the words came out as a massive bubble and her whole life flashed before her eyes as he pushed her down again and the water went up her nose and filled her mouth with a salty tang. She could not breathe. She struggled but vainly as the man had assumed the strength of Goliath and she realised she was drowning…

Suddenly, a commotion above her head spun her round and she found herself free and able to stand up, gasping for air and holding her side which felt as though it had been pierced. Hitting into her attacker was the soldier she had spurned and criticised, earlier on the sea road. However, as fast as he hit the man, his fists went through and the demon laughed and laughed and eventually disappeared, leaving Verity and her saviour face to face.
"Where the hell did you come from?" she cried breathlessly, conscious that her language was hardly that of a refined lady.

The soldier laughed and hemmed at her outburst and told her, more to the point, where the hell did that thing come from?

"He is a demon set to distract me from my path of discovery and send me straight to my death," she told her saviour.
His eyes widened and the two of them waded out of the sea and onto some rocks that were dry and at a safe distance from the waves.

The ouzel bird turned his beak to the south west and had a quick preen of his feathers, making sure every one was in fine fettle.
Two miles to go! Sang his tiny heart. Then I can rest.
The letter was tucked under his wing and he took off again with a thrilling wave of song that flooded the firmaments and pushed him on down the last green valley.
After another hour he came to the monastery gates and saw, in the garden there, two of the brothers hoeing vegetables and clearing the weeds.
"Brother Adam! Brother Adam!" he sang sweetly from the bough of a nearby apple tree that was pushing out its leaves.
The tallest of the monks raised his head and asked who called him and why.
"It is I, the magical ouzel bird," came back the reply from the greening bough.
Adam looked in amazement at the bird and as he drew near, a letter with his name on it fell to the earth at his feet. He picked it up and tore open the paper, reading the missive inside with smiling lips and a happy heart.
Verity! He thought. She was safe...at least for now.

He read the letter at least twice and then, pocketing the missive in his habit, he turned to the ouzel bird, still perched on the branch of the tree. The bird's bright eye followed him everywhere.
"You have done well, my friend, and shown true courage and strength in the face of adversity! What a dark and arduous journey you must have had! Rest must follow and Verity orders me to find you a safe and warm corner of our garden here to live."

"My power flits and fades," crooned the bird, "The magic drains from me like the turning tide and I shall soon be what I was...a dumb ouzel bird who can, nevertheless, sing his heart out when the sun rises in the sky! I am happy with your plan and shall remain here!" and he folded his wings in resignation.

Adam looked and looked again. The magic had drained from the black and white plumage and he was what he said he would become, a pied ouzel bird who could sing from dawn to dusk.

A melodious song escaped his beak as he rose up and flew with Brother Adam to find the sanctuary that he so deserved.

The tide was on the turn. Slowly the white chargers eased their attack on the beach and the noise of water on sand and gravel subsided. Verity felt embarrassed now her stupidity had been exposed.

What did Adam say to me, she queried, as they sat, waiting for the beach to be exposed once more. There will be many sent to distract you from your path and you must be wary. It seems I have let outward appearances seduce and flatter me…

The soldier was speaking now.

"I said I only have dried meat in my bag to offer you and I know that is not to your taste."

Verity shook her head.

"It is no matter," she replied. "I am not hungry."

"I could catch you some fish from the retreating waves or we could pull some mussels from the rocks that I see peering from the water."

Again, Verity shook her head.

"I do not eat anything living," she told the man, "They will not die for my plate. Talk fruit, bread or grains and I am with you but warm, living flesh...no."

She lapsed into thought then, suddenly conscious she was being rude, she plunged into conversation once more.

"You saved my life and I do not even know your name."

"Andrew," he told her, "Andrew Parr. And it was indeed a pleasure to rescue you from the clutches of...that thing. I must be honest, the incident has shocked me. I thought the man flesh but my fists went straight through him."

"He was a demon and I was warned of his coming," mused Verity, "Yet I picked the wrong one."

Andrew pulled a face.

"You thought me a demon then?" he queried.

Verity was conscious she had been very rude.

"Er...that is...yes. I thought it likely...well possible."

"Because I offered you what you think of as dead flesh?"

Verity shrugged.

"Perhaps," she said, "I thought it strange that you were walking out this way at the same time as I was. I worried you had been sent to destroy me..."

"With meat?" he asked, but there was a smile on his face as he said it.

Verity actually laughed. She felt easier now in his company and very soon, they could see the rocks, which half an hour ago were completely submerged by the sea.

"I think that is where my prize lies," Verity told Andrew.

"Your prize? May I ask what game this is you are playing?"

"You may ask but I cannot tell you. I walk a lonely road and no-one must go with me. It is no game but life and death to my fiancé."

"Ah…love," replied the young man, "There is no path a woman will not tread for that. Nor a man either. So, what is your prize on those rocks?"

Reluctantly Verity told him.

"You have heard of these rare periwinkles?" she asked.

"Yes...and seen them in my childhood too but there are few left now to grace the seaweed ribbons on the rocks."

"You think my journey here futile then?"

"Oh no – I am sure we will find one or two among the more common whelks and barnacles."

"You come from here then? You were brought up here?"

"Yes, a few miles away. I went for a soldier but it was not to my liking so I bought my way out when my father died and took over his business to provide for my three sisters and my mother."

"You look like a soldier," replied Verity, dreamily, "You have the upright bearing of a military man. How sad to have to leave such a romantic occupation and return to the mere drudgery of a business!"

Andrew shook his head.

"I do not see it that way," he affirmed, "I am happy to take the reins and provide for my family."

After another half an hour, Verity judged she could wade out to the rocks and search for her second prize. Andrew was anxious to accompany her but she told him she had to do this alone.

"That's as may be but I can watch from afar and then come to your rescue should you get into any difficulties."

She agreed with that and removed her shoes and stockings, ready to begin her search. However, after reaching the water's edge she turned back and shrugged her shoulders in despair.

"I do not know what this periwinkle looks like," she wailed, "It has to be the correct one or the witch will never give me the jewels I need to barter with the dragon! And any delay is so dangerous as Lawrence may kill my beloved! Oh I hope and pray that the ouzel bird made it safely to the monastery!"

Andrew did not understand all of which she spoke but he could see she was upset and he came forward and found a short stick which he drew with in the shallow sand.

"Here is the snail," he told her, "See how his shell curls once, twice, three times while the other more common snails have only one convolution! You cannot miss his colour, it is as pink as the sunset and he is much larger than the other drab snails who have brown or grey shells."

Verity thanked him and made her way through the water to the exposed rocks. They were slippery with seaweed and still wet so she had to take great care. Small whirling rock pools were forming as the tide left the area and retreated so she began to scrutinise these and search for a pink snail who was larger than his brothers. All the snails she saw were small and of light brown hue so she knew they were no good.

Climbing over the rocks to the far pool she suddenly spotted one, just one, who stood out among his fellows like a peacock among hens.

"I have found the periwinkle!" she cried, turning to her companion who stood at the shore's edge watching her.

She took the tiny creature in her hand and turned him over but her heart was hit by a terrible truth. He would die if she took him with her and, besides, she only needed his shell. She replaced him in the water and made her way back to the shore.

Andrew was perplexed.

"What is the matter?" he asked, "Why did you not bring the shell?"

Verity shook her head.

"There was a life in there," she told him, "I have to perform these acts with compassion. If I drag him from the sea in his house, then he will die. I cannot have murder on my hands, no matter what. The ouzel bird feather was obtained with kindness and this has to be done in the same way."

Andrew looked at her in sheer amazement.

"What can we do then?" he murmured.

It seemed the second prize was on hold.

CHAPTER NINE

Verity wandered up and down the shoreline, hands on hips, thinking deeply.
It is but a mollusc, said her head and the pain it will feel, if any, is inconsequential as to what Frederick feels.
It is a life, said her heart, and nothing will be achieved by murdering this life for another.

She turned to her companion and saw the quizzical expression on his face. After another minute or two of thought her face brightened.
"We must find another shell," she said, at length, "One that is bigger and finer than the pink house he lives in."
"He'?" queried Andrew, in confusion, "Can a snail be a 'he'?"

Verity shrugged.
"I don't know," she said, "However, I do know that he or she is alive and will feel pain if I remove them from the water and then they will die and I will be a murderer."

Andrew was very puzzled.
"You need that shell you said, as your prize, so surely that comes before anything? The death of one snail, rare or not, will surely not condemn you?"

Verity sighed.
"It does in my eyes," she said, "Time presses, Andrew, so please help me search for another shell, finer than the one the creature inhabits and I can ask him to move!"

Andrew looked even more incredulous but he did as she asked him and they searched the nearby rock pools. It was he that found a splendid pale grey shell, larger than the pink one Verity had found and thicker too.
"Will this do?" he asked her, handing her the empty object.

Verity checked it thoroughly for signs of life and nodded. She strode back to the pool where she had found the periwinkle and noticed that Andrew followed her.
"I must go alone," she reminded him when she reached the pool. He acknowledged her request and stopped, turning

back a little, but still keeping his eyes on her form for fear other demons crossed her path.

Verity picked up the periwinkle and admired his pastel colour.

"Dear friend," she said, "I have a favour to ask of you, not for my sake but for the sake of someone I love. I need your shell for the witch as you are so rare but I would not dream of taking it whilst you inhabit it. SO, I have brought you another shell, not so beautiful I must admit but bigger and thicker and just as suitable for you to live in. Will you change homes and help me?"

The snail in her hand quivered and then the answer came back to her, high and shrill, as though on the wind from the salty waves.

"You have shown me compassion so I will help you. You could have taken me out of my rock pool, bigger and stronger as you are, and just let me die in the air. You would thus have had my shell and that is all you want. However, you have brought me a bigger and better shell and I can change homes if you put me near and thus keep my life. I will do as you ask."

Verity was delighted.

"Bless you, tiny life," she said, "You still have the right to live in peace and I am sorry to disturb you but on this shell depends another life. I shall put this larger home close to you now and wait for you to leave your present one."

She did as the snail asked and watched, fascinated, as he wriggled out of the periwinkle shell and crawled into the larger grey one.

"And are you happy in there?" she asked him as he settled into the new dimensions of the shell.

"Yes," he replied, "Please put me back in the rock pool and I can move around and live my life in peace. Yes, you may have disturbed me but I can survive in this shell and I know now I have done a good thing."

Verity took the empty shell and kissed it.

"You have done a great thing," she said, "You have saved a life and, as such, I am forever in your debt."

"As you spared me and let me live I can grant one wish for you," said the snail, "Then my power will flit and fade...what would you like me to do for you?"

Verity thought of her next prize and of the veil of mystery that surrounded it.

"I do not know how I shall move on from here and find the county where my next prize comes from," she said, "Does your magic tell you where I must go?"

The snail moved back and forth as though rocking and said,

"Yes, I know of what you speak and, even though you must solve the riddle for yourself, I can fly you to the county of Carmarthenshire which is where you need to be."

"Fly me?" queried Verity. "How can you do that?"

The snail rocked and rocked and said, in his high shrill voice,

"You shall see!"

The view from the back of the giant albatross was spectacular. Over fields, rivers and woods the giant bird flew and Verity hung on to his neck as his massive wings flapped and he soared high on air currents above the Welsh countryside. Gradually, the coast disappeared as they flew inland and Andrew was just a spot on the beach.

"Goodbye! Goodbye!" he called as the bird took off from a high rock.

From Verity, a wave of the hand and a grateful cry,

"Goodbye! Thank you so much for helping me!"

They flew and flew and the sun went down and came up again and she knew another day had passed in the grip of magic. The sky was red and then dark and then blue and high, mighty clouds brought rain and then a flurry of sleet that sparkled like diamonds in the cooling air.

Verity shivered and drew her cloak around her but just then, the bird began to descend and down, down, down they went and the air suddenly became warm and humid. The albatross landed in a small clearing in a forest and bowed to his passenger as she got off.

"Madam, my time for speech is short for the magic that has taken over me wanes with the rising of the sun. I thank you for your compassion to the tiniest life form...the periwinkle...and it has brought you great riches in that your third prize grows here in profusion."

"Where are we?" asked Verity, looking round her.

"You are in Carmarthenshire," replied the bird with a wave of his wing. "A magical county where Myrddin, the Druid, casts his nets of spells. Caerfyrddin is the fortress of Merlin and you may indeed come across him in these woods as he wanders, searching for precious herbs and potions. I must leave you now for my power flits and fades. Goodbye Verity! Goodbye!" and the enormous albatross unfolded his wings and took off into the wind. She saw him circle on the freshets and then he headed back to the coast.

"Goodbye, albatross and thank you!" she called.

"My third prize grows in woodland dells
Surrounded by a Druid's spells,
Brave yellow and encased in green
Within this county, only seen
Where brave Carmarthen raises rain
Adorning now a true Welsh lane,
A beauty bright upon the eye
So look, look hard but don't pass by,
The Derwydd grows in this fair soil
To find his bloom is your next toil.
But not his leaves and not his bud
His bulb you must dig from the mud
So rare now for a witches' spell
Search in the hollows and green dells
But beware, to Merlin these belong
And each is counted in his song
Be courteous and smile and bow
And one rare bulb he may allow...."

Verity read the riddle through twice and light dawned in her tired mind.

A daffodil, she thought. A fair flower that is green and yellow and often tinged with orange. It sounded easy and she folded the paper and put it in her bag. Turning to the woods again, she cast her eyes this way and that but no flowers were visible, save a few early windflowers.

They are not my prize, she said to herself and, shouldering her bag, she began to wander through the trees. Her eyes were on the floor where an autumn of leaves remained decomposing gently and a few shoots of bracken or ling pushed their way through, for it was May and the season when new life was beginning to show.

Will there be daffodils, she wondered? Will I find flowers or just dying green leaves and what if I dig up the wrong bulbs and take them to the witch? Will I be sent back to find the right one or will that be it for my beloved? No second chance, no return to this secluded spot? How would I ever find it again and…

Her reverie was interrupted by the crunch of leaves and the shout of a loud voice,

"Who are you and what are you doing in my wood?"

Verity jumped and turned around to behold a huge man with a long black beard and a mop of unruly black curls upon his head. He was quite seven foot and the tallest person she had ever seen. Peering out from the face were sharp blue eyes and in his hand the man carried a staff, much like the one she had safely brought all the way from the monastery. She instinctively took a step back.

"Frightened of me, are you?" bellowed the man as he took a few steps forward. He towered over her but she remembered her quest and stood up straight and strong.

"I am Verity Whittle and my quest here is to find the Derwydd and obtain a bulb to go with my other prizes!"

The man screwed up his face and regarded her sharply.

"A common thief, eh? And who told you there were Derwydds growing in my woods!"

Verity was a little confused,

"The periwinkle did," she replied truthfully, "He summoned the albatross and I flew here on giant wings!"

The man never moved but looked her up and down as though doubting her story.
"Do you know who I am?" he asked presently.
"No," she said, "However, I can see you are a great fighter and also a landowner, seeing as this wood is yours. Therefore, I appeal to your kind and generous nature to let me dig up just one bulb!"

The man threw back his head and laughed.
"Why, you are nothing more than a common peasant!" he roared, "I am the great Merlin, Druid warrior of this region and you are still trespassing on my land!"
"Sire...I am sorry. The albatross brought me here and my quest involves life or death..."
"For a flower, ma'am, or should I say a bulb? The fact remains that you wish to rape my woodland and damage the rare daffodil that I protect with my life!"

Verity was getting exasperated.
"I only wish for one bulb," she begged. "Not to save my own life but that of my beloved."

The giant warrior wandered back and forth, considering her request and stroking his luxurious beard.
"You do know the Derwydd is Wales' rarest flower?" he snorted, "One bulb gone means one less to produce a daffodil next spring! What if I said to all comers, 'Come into my woodland and dig up the rarest of the rare for your garden!' What if I said that, madam? The Derwydd would be non-existent here!"
"Yet prolific and much loved in many a Welsh garden, sir!"

The great Merlin stared. He had obviously not seen the problem from that angle.
"Ah...but I would not be able to see them and they are the flower of my county!"
"Perhaps, sir, they would spread far and wide throughout Wales if they were to be transplanted? Think of that...the Derwydd in every part of Wales!"

Merlin did not like that concept.

"They have only ever grown in Carmarthen soil," he bellowed, "So where are you taking your bulb and will it be replanted?"

Verity felt the conversation was getting increasingly complicated but she hung on,
"I don't know, sir, that I don't. I know the bulb would be used, that is for sure. Do not forget though I only crave ONE."
"So where will it be going?" asked Merlin, bending down to gaze into her face, "You have not said."
"It goes to a witch, sir, in another part of the country, for her spells. I need it to swap for jewels for the dragon."
"Ha," cried Merlin, his hands twirling the staff he carried, "You think you will get an audience with the dragon? Why, he will take a breath and blow flames to roast you to a crisp!"
"That is a chance I am prepared to take, sir, for the man I love!"

Silence fell.
"The staff you carry," murmured the Druid, "Where did you obtain it from? It looks familiar."
"Brother Adam Curlious gave it to me, sir, or rather his father did. Brother Adam has completed the task I am given and he obtained the heart of his father which was bound to a vampire."

Merlin scratched his head.
"A monk?" he said, "A monk who came this way a little while ago and also tried to rape my woodland?"
"Yes, sir, but he is a man of God and as such, his heart is pure and he would have wanted the Derwydd to save the life of his father. I need it to save the life of my betrothed. We both have travelled the same path but I have two more prizes to win after this one and if I fail, my beloved slips through my fingers. My happiness, sir, depends on one bulb!"

Merlin traced a heart with the base of his staff in the woodland earth,
"So I stand here, the great Myrddin, with a woman's future in my hands!"

Verity sensed he was weakening and pressed on.
"You do, sir, and such a great warrior as yourself would never knowingly stand in the way of my success, surely? It is such a little request!"
"Hmm...I am not without compassion but the Derwydd..."
"Are they blooming still, sir, or have the flowers faded on the stem?"
"Most have a day or two of beauty left," the great man replied, "I should not want them plucked from the earth until their green had faded..."
"Neither would I. All my prizes have to be won with complete compassion," and she told him of the ouzel bird and the rare periwinkle and what she had done.

Merlin looked pensive.
"And your name?" he asked, "I know you introduced yourself but remind me again as I like to know who I am dealing with."
"Verity Whittle, sir," and she held out her hand to him, "Do we have a deal, sir? I wait for the Derwydd and then take just one bulb when the green has withered from the stem?"

The Druid looked deep into her eyes and pronounced that, despite being a woman, she had the heart and soul of a warrior. He drew back a little but then came forward towards her again.
"I remember now that Brother Adam and he was a cultured gentleman from my own country. He brought me seeds from a beautiful plant that now graces my castle garden. And you say he liked and approved of you?"
"Yes, sir. It was he who told of the magic and sent me on this journey, knowing, no doubt, that you would be here to help me."

Merlin looked pleased at this and drew himself up to full height.
"He placed his trust in you," continued Verity, sensing she was very near her prize.
"So be it," said the great man and extended his huge hand to hers. They shook.
The Derwydd was within Verity's grasp.

The small bower, full of gentle green light, was a joy to behold. Verity followed Merlin down the winding path and saw, scattered about in a haphazard pattern, many daffodils with huge trumpets and delicate leaves, some so see-through that the earth beyond them was visible. Many were just on the point of surrendering their beauty but some had blooms that were yet to open.

"Oh this is delightful!" she enthused, stroking the waving flowers and gazing about.

"It is my special place," the Druid told her, pleased at her obvious enthusiasm for his bower.

"I brought Brother Adam here and he too expressed happiness at the peace of the place. Like you he trod the path of compassion."

"It is the only way," Verity told him. "I vowed from a child that no living being, however small, should suffer for my existence and I keep to it. I will wait till the flowers die off and not disturb the Derwydd till its beauty dies."

"One plant, mind you!" shouted Merlin, almost deafening Verity as he stood close.

"Of course," she replied, meekly bowing her head, "I would like you to choose since they are your special flowers."

"They grow nowhere outside my home county," he told her, as he scanned the yellow heads, "They are precious beyond measure and even the departure of one bulb fills me with sorrow."

"If there was another way, I would take it," Verity reassured him, "I will perform the task with utmost compassion, be assured of that."

"Hmm...I think this one has sadly seen better days but mind you leave it until the flower's yellow has drifted into brown. I will be back to check."

Verity nodded,

"I will wait here until the flower has given up its beautiful colour and then I will dig that bulb up, but only that one, you can be assured."

"The great Merlin has many things to do and cannot wait but I will return in three days when, I judge, this bloom will be dead and the act can be performed, under my supervision of course. I would prefer to do it since this is my wood and my land!"

Verity acquiesced at once. It was a small price to pay for the Derwydd and her third prize captured.

She made herself comfortable in the warm, green bower and looked around her. The small trees and bushes shaded her from the hot May sun and a fragrant breeze reached her, smelling of all that spring can offer in country regions. Then, gradually, a voice reached her ears and she looked around her with some nervousness. Surely Merlin had gone? No, it was far too high pitched for his gruff tones and not a soul was visible. She got up to survey her surroundings better. "You humans really are dense at times!" came the squeaky voice again, "I am sure plants have bigger brains and far more common sense! It is ME talking, the flower you intend digging up once my beauty has faded!"

Verity looked and looked again and found herself incredulous.

"Can you really speak to me?" she asked in breathless tones, homing in on the Derwydd who rocked gently in the breeze as he spoke.

"Only for a short while and, I must say, I am glad of that, seeing as you seem to possess the intelligence of a weed!"

Verity found herself apologising to the daffodil.

"I am sorry I have to disturb you, I am sorry I have to dig you up," she began.

The flower waved his green leaves.

"It is of no matter," he said, "At least you are leaving me to enjoy my beauty for another couple of days and not dragging me, screaming and protesting from the soil!"

"Oh, I would never do that!" replied Verity, deeply shocked.

"Well, others have ventured into these woods and done just that in other springs. Sometimes we can barely lift our heads and we are plucked from our resting places and stuffed into an earthenware jar. They forget the water, oh yes, they often

forget the water or leave it to go green and foul. I ask you, would you like to drink that?"
"No," said Verity, still somewhat amazed that she was talking to a daffodil. Recovering a little she asked the flower if it hurt to be plucked from the soil.
"Not really," came the squeaky reply, "I can't say it is pleasant but I do not feel what you would describe as pain. Still, Myrddin guards us to the best of his ability when we are in bud and flower."
"I would never dream of taking a bud," Verity told him, "A little bird told me you are rare too!"
"Ha ha!" laughed the Derwydd, "I would not describe Myrddin as little or bird-like but yes, we are very rare and we only grow on Carmarthenshire soil, which is where you stand now!"

Verity tried to engage the flower in more conversation about his life but he said he was tired now and shook his leaves out a little and went to sleep.

Three days, thought Verity as she covered herself with her cloak later when darkness had fallen and the woodland was full of strange noises. Yet I would do three years for you, Frederick, and hardly blink an eye. She looked up at the space in the canopy and thought the stars were looking down on her and blessing her in her travels. The moon rose, huge and luminous and the night creatures began their search for food. Surprisingly, Verity found she was not frightened and her last picture of the day was Frederick, standing whole and well, as she last saw him, when he left for Wales.

CHAPTER TEN

Verity woke, somewhat refreshed, and found the flower was stretching and yawning too as he opened his trumpet to the first light of the dawn.

"The darkness is gone!" he squeaked. "The sun is up and my roots are feeding from the rich loam soil underneath."

"Do you require anything?" asked Verity, drinking the last of the water that kind Rose had packed for her. Now the bottle was empty.

"Is there a stream anywhere near?" she asked her yellow and green companion, who looked even more beautiful as the sun gilded his golden petals.

"Yes, over to the left of the bower, and a little of that water would refresh me too, if you don't mind."

Verity got up and stretched her stiff body and, climbing out of the bower, a shine of water caught her eye and the pleasant sound of trickling liquid invigorated her senses. She hastened over to the stream and washed her face and hands, drying them on a large pocket handkerchief she had had the presence of mind to bring with her. She filled the two bottles she carried and went back to the bower where she emptied half the contents of one over the flower.

"That's enough!" squeaked the dissatisfied plant, "It may rain later so don't overdo it. No nuts for you to eat and you can't get nutriments from the soil like I do."

"I still have some bread," said Verity hopefully, but the end of the loaf was too hard to bite. Instead, to take her mind off the gnawing hunger, she found her comb and tidied her tangled hair, removing a few leaves and a quantity of twigs.

An hour later Merlin burst into the clearing and called her name.

"Miss Whittle! Miss Whittle!"

"Here, sir," she called, jumping up. She climbed out of the bower and found him with a sack over his shoulder.

"Ah," he mused, "I did think you were a figment of my imagination yesterday and that you would roll away with the spring mist! Yet you stand in front of me, as much flesh and blood as myself! I have brought you some food!"

"It is very kind of you, sir," replied Verity, dreading to think what was in the sack but trying to be grateful.

The Druid unloaded the goods he had bought and, as Verity had feared, it was nothing her compassion would let her eat.

"Dried rabbit, hare stew and some mead to wash it all down with," he said, "My servants made it for you today after breakfast was cleared. Well, my girl, why don't you appear more grateful? Are you not hungry then?"

Verity felt very awkward.

"I am hungry, yes, I am, sir but not for foods like that which once lived and had a face and a life. I will not eat of the flesh of others, slaughtered to give me a meal, when I do not need to."

"What nonsense is this?" roared the great man, "You refuse to eat my specially prepared food? Why, what ails it?"

Verity drew herself up to her fullest height.

"What ails it, sir, as you put it, is that living beings died to produce it. I am not a murderer, sir, and neither do I want anyone else to murder on my behalf. I cannot eat any of it nor drink the mead either as that is made with honey and that belongs to the bees. We have no right to rape their hives and take it!"

Merlin was deeply shocked. No one had ever stood up to him like this before. All bowed down to him in the county and his word was law. He did not know what to say.

"Food to me is not dead, rotting carcases that man has killed to fill his belly. Food to me is the plant kingdom or the grains we grow in the fields and make into bread or pancakes. My maid Liddy makes the most delicious cakes with flour, sugar, oil and water plus fruits but she does not use pieces of animals men have killed! I would rather go hungry for the three days I am here than eat the decaying flesh you bring me!"

Merlin looked at the food. He was confused it was true but a part of him wanted to hear more of this peculiar viewpoint.

"So I must return to my castle and bring you...what?" he asked.

Waiting for the furious backlash, Verity was amazed at the calmness of his voice.

"It is my religion, sir, not to eat anything from an animal and I have been hale and hearty from it all these years. The God I worship exists in Nature and animals are my equals...He teaches me that."

"Does He indeed," mumbled Merlin, feeling somewhat out of his depths as to how this conversation was proceeding.

"What shall I bring you then, Miss Whittle? Bread and water?"

"Water I have, sir, from the stream over there but my bread is dry and hard."

"Fresh bread then and what else?"

"Do you have any nuts, sir, or any fruit?"

"Yes, we stored some hazelnuts from last autumn and apples too. Why, you are a squirrel, Miss Whittle!"

Verity smiled.

"Maybe I am, sir," she replied, "Maybe I am."

It was two hours later and the day was advancing. Merlin had returned to his castle and given orders to his housekeeper to rustle up anything edible that did not come from an animal.

"Is that not impossible, sir?" she had asked him, "In all my years serving you, I have never been asked such a thing before!"

"Bread," replied the Druid, "Bread and fruit and nuts. Do you have all that?"

"Yes, sir, we do. Russets wrapped in paper stored in the larder and hazelnuts in shells on the pantry shelf ready for nut pudding."

"Good," replied the great man, "Send the cook to me too, for I want her to make some cakes but not as she usually does, cracking ten eggs. These must be flour, sugar, oil and fruit."

True, the cook threatened to leave over her unusual orders that day but an extra guinea kept her happy and Merlin

carried the cakes, hot and fragrant, back to the bower for his young guest. He watched her eat with an amused expression on his face.
"So how do you feel now, Miss Whittle?" he asked, when some of the cakes were gone and the nuts and bread and she was starting on an apple.
"Satisfied, sir, as regards my hunger and virtuous in my soul that no lives were lost in the making of my meal."
"Hmm...I shall have to try one of these cakes. Mine contain at least ten eggs and cost a pretty penny too!"

He bit into one of the sweetmeats and ate the cake in two bites.
"So how do you feel now, great Merlin?" asked Verity as she finished her fruit.

The huge man got up and looked down on her as she sat. "Lighter in the belly," was his reply.

Verity smiled. The humorous moments on her path kept her mind from straying to the dungeon where Frederick languished and from the fact that two more prizes had to be won before she could even think of seeing him again.

The next two days passed swiftly and the weather was kind, as warm and fragrant as May can make the woodlands, and Merlin called once a day with food for his guest, and often ate it with her, although he worried how she would ever gain strength for the next leg of her journey on such a diet.
"It may be light, sir, but it is nourishing and gives me the energy I need to push onwards with the bulb when you decree that day has come."

The flower himself acknowledged he was fading and the yellow was drifting into brown but he craved another day and Verity gave it to him. However, on the morrow, he had sunk to the earth and his life force, he admitted, was descending into the bulb. Finally, Merlin, who could not hear his message as that was directed for Verity's ears only, brought a small spade and dug up the prize, rubbing the bulb free of excess dirt before he put it in Verity's hand.

"The third prize!" she exclaimed, gleefully, "Two more and I have what the witch needs to turn into jewels and woo the dragon!"
"Good luck with that," huffed Merlin, knowing dragons are very fickle and temperamental.

The next morning Verity took leave of the bower and walked from the sheltered woodland with her staff and her precious prizes wrapped, for safety, in her bag. However, as she left, she heard a voice emanating from her bag and she realised it was the Derwydd trying to call her. She took out the bulb and turned it to the light. A small face appeared in the earthy object and squeaked to her,
"I promised you a favour for the days you left me to enjoy my blooms and now has come the time I must give it. What do you require?"

Verity thought for a moment. Only that morning had she turned to the parchment and read the next clue to the third prize.

"You have found three, so four will follow
But seek a tree that's dead and hollow
For that is where your next prize lies
He warms himself beneath Welsh skies
Cold of blood and green of skin
Long is his body but also quite thin,
On Welsh soil now he rears his head
His bite, I fear, could mean you're dead
Devouring insects with great delight
He slithers by day and also by night
Rare as the unicorn creature is he
And two of these you'll never see
But one small snake, he may be found
Where water cools the marshy ground
Or forest lair, brings leaves to hide
But watch your feet, step to one side
You need his skin, so rare, so green
He hides away, is rarely seen
But you must grasp him, poison too

The rest is really up to you..."

Verity read the verse to the Derwydd and waited for his response.
"Do you know what creature this is I must seek and where I can find him?" she asked, suddenly anxious she was on her own with this problem.
The Derwydd pulled a face.
"Snakes!" he spat, "Yes, they have slithered past me in all my spring glory but not this particular one as he does not frequent the soils of Carmarthenshire. However, head north from here up into mid Wales and ask there for a lady called Sarah White. She used to come to the woodland and measure and study there and she knew all about the Davion, which is the snake you seek. She lives in a hamlet called Fouracres and you will find it a few miles north of here. If you become lost, ask for her and her house which is called Fourwinds. I wish you luck and now I will become what I was, as my magic flits and fades. Goodbye!"
"Goodbye, brave Derwydd!" cried Verity, kissing his small brown face but when she looked again all she held in her hand was a flower bulb. She wrapped it tenderly, put it in her bag and changed her path to a northerly one.

She walked for a couple of hours and noticed the countryside changing slowly but surely. The valleys were more pronounced and she struggled up higher hills and admired the luxurious views from the summits. Wave upon wave of green, rolling leas, vales and here and there a tract of woodland. She stopped at lunch time and ate some of the bread and fruit Merlin had given her for the journey and she drank of a bower stream and found it sweet and cool. It was hot now and she put her cloak aside and was grateful for the staff to steady her steps. She peered at the Derwydd again as she ate, as though she expected him to renew his face but he was merely a dark brown bulb and she found she missed his chatter.

"You gave your life for me really, although I tried to show what compassion I could and allowed you those sweet spring days to enjoy! I hope the witch will plant you and, with water and warmth, you will bloom again, though in foreign climes."

She was descending another steep hill and her side ached, so she stopped to stretch and rest and found herself overtaken by another woman, almost equal in age and height to herself.

"Good afternoon!" cried the stranger as she breezed past.

Verity replied, then thought deeply and called after the woman who slowed her walk and turned round.

"Can I help you?" she asked, walking back towards Verity.
"I am looking for a hamlet called Fouracres and a house called Fourwinds," Verity told her, "There a lady called Sarah White lives who I need to see on urgent business."
"What business is that?" asked the woman, and Verity noticed she carried a large jar on her hip.
"I - I cannot say," replied Verity, suddenly feeling awkward.
"It is no matter as I do not know the woman," replied her new acquaintance, "However, I know the hamlet you talk of and I am walking that way, so we may as well go together."

Verity agreed and they continued on their way. It was good to have some female company and Verity admitted she missed the muddle-headed chat of her maid.
'What is Liddy doing as I walk these paths?' she thought, 'Has she taken good care of my Jet? For, along with Frederick, he is the most important living being in my life.'

The woman, who said her name was Brighty, was asking lots of questions but Verity felt rather uneasy revealing anything about her journey, so she was very vague and feigned indifference most of the time.
"What do you have in the jar?" she asked her companion, in order to change the subject.
"Seed potatoes which I am taking to my mother, that she may plant them out and grow yet more. They are the finest in all of Wales!"

Verity was glad to be on a safer subject and she let the woman prattle on about growing vegetables and fruit. They climbed many hills and yet never seemed to get any nearer the elusive interior of Wales. At length Verity declared they were going the wrong way.
"How can you know that seeing as you have never been to Fouracres before?" asked the girl, throwing down the jar and taking a rest on the edge of a steep slope.
"I was given directions and they were very precise," replied Verity, sitting down also, as the climb had exhausted her, "I must leave you now and peruse the track I was told to take."

Barely were those words out of her mouth, when the woman had attacked her and the two rolled over and over, getting perilously near to the edge of the precipice. Verity did not have time to feel fear, she put every inch of her strength into keeping her head from going over the cliff. At one point her adversary's eyes were visible and they were blood red, so Verity knew she was facing a she-devil of the worst kind. Slowly, Verity felt she was getting the upper hand but the harpy screamed out,
"Bethel! Bethel! Leave your jar and come and help me!"

To her horror, Verity saw a tiny demon, out of the corner of her eye, crawl from the leaning jar and make his way towards them both. He began to bite Verity's ankles and she screamed and kicked out.

Yet again, she was close to the cliff edge and she closed her eyes and expected to feel the sensation of falling. Frederick's face flashed into her brain but, miraculously, the hands upon her loosened and she heard blow after blow reigning down around her but never touching her person. She judged it to be with her own staff and the two devils were obviously the recipients of the blows but she rolled herself up into a ball and wondered if she were next.

Silence, save for her own rapid breathing and her heartbeat racing in her ears. She sensed someone was leaning over her but she dared not open her eyes to look.
"All right you evil bastard," she shouted, "Do your worst and throw me over the edge!"

Silence...and then a somewhat offended voice said,
"Well, I rescue you for a second time and save your life and this is how you repay me!"
Andrew, said her exhausted brain. Andrew! But how?

She felt him lifting her away from the cliff edge and she opened her eyes in amazement.
"Did you really think I was going to let you just fly away on the unluckiest of birds, the giant albatross, and disappear into the blue? Why, just touching that bird probably called those demons up!"
"You followed me!"
He smiled.
"Well, it wasn't difficult," he admitted, "I already knew where you were heading for and as you were there a few days I soon caught you up. But that Druid! I kept out of his way, for sure."

Exhaustion suddenly overcame Verity and she collapsed upon the ground.
"I got the Derwydd," she said in a small, weak voice and then the world went black.

She woke up, many hours later and found she was cocooned in Andrew's cloak. She felt confused and then reality came back to her. The she-devil and Bethel! She gave a gasp and found her saviour was at her side.
"You must have had some disturbing dreams," he told her, "You groaned and moaned and I was worried you would roll over the cliff and finish the job the devils started!"
Verity rubbed her head.
"It is not funny," she murmured, still feeling dazed. She looked down at the cloak that covered her. Silver and blue! She had not noticed Andrew wearing it when he came upon her.
"This..." and she pointed. Andrew gently unwrapped her and folded the cloak up.
"Er...just something I happened to find on my journey," he commented, "I expect you will want to be on your way now you have joined the world again."

Verity felt puzzled.

"Ah, yes," she said, "Fouracres and the search for Sarah White. However, I must travel alone and leave you here as you know the rules and, were I to break them, my beloved could be lost to me!"

"He would not be, as I..." Andrew's voice broke off. He stopped himself saying anything further and finished with, "As I will not follow you any more."

"You promise?"

"I don't make promises but you have my word as a mere mortal."

Verity stood up.

"Very well," she said, "That is good enough for me. I must trust you I suppose. So what are you going to do now?"

Andrew shrugged.

"Have a sleep on this verdant pasture before returning to my homeland."

"Which is?" queried Verity.

"Wherever I decide to go."

"But your family...the one you are supporting? You said you were working to keep them and had had to leave the army!"

Andrew looked embarrassed.

"Ah...yes...that. Well, happen I have brought the business back from the brink and can be spared a few days on a jaunt!"

"So that is what my life and death journey is to you!" she joked, picking up her bag and checking all the items in it were intact.

"Oh no," he cried, in earnest. "It is far, far more than that to me!"

Verity smiled but knew the day had advanced and she must be on her way.

"Goodbye, Andrew!" she said, stepping up to him and giving him her hand. She saw the beautiful cloak was lying on the grass at his feet and she felt a power emanating from it that confused her. How could that be?

She left him with some regret and, turning, saw he was watching her closely. She waved and then the path took her out of sight.

It was an hour later that she got the sudden urge to return to the scene of her attack. It overcame her so strongly she could hardly breathe.

Is Andrew in trouble, her heart cried. You must retrace your footsteps, said her wise head. It was so rare that they were in agreement that she turned and began to climb the track she had lately come down.

After a while she came to the ridge where her life had been saved and she saw Andrew laying on the grass, sweetly asleep. She could hear his gentle snores and she crept up on him with a smile on her face. The blue and silver cloak lay all around him and his face looked so angelic as he breathed in and out, in and out. Angelic...oh my God, she cried inwardly, suddenly seeing what sprouted from his back as he lay on the sparkling garment.

Wings! WINGS! Huge, soft, feathered wings in pure white...wings…

Suddenly, she knew how he had followed her from the coast and why he had appeared in her life twice now, both times when she was in grave danger. A fragment from Mr Curlious came back to her that he had almost whispered as she left,

"The road will be frequented by devils, it is true, but the Blessed Ones look down and they can intervene if your life is truly in danger! Remember that!"

She had forgotten it. In the dark pictures of the evil that haunted the road, she had forgotten what existed on the other side, the side of right and justice and goodness. She was being followed by an angel and he had the cloak of St Michael to protect her. No wonder she had recovered so quickly from the attack! No wonder she felt the healing power of the garment when she stepped near it. Andrew had not trailed the many miles she had over hill and valley. He had flown!

She brushed away a tear and left the sleeping angel for the road to Fouracres. She was safe now.

CHAPTER ELEVEN

Verity pressed onwards, following the instructions she had been given and, apart from a small ache in her side, totally recovered from her ordeal. She felt, in her heart, it had been worth the pain to see Andrew's soul laid bare and she could not resist, every so often, looking skywards to see if he was following her.

His promise was meaningless, she told herself, for had he not declared he was a mere mortal, when, in fact, he grappled with immortality? He was the alter ego to the bloodsuckers she was trying to oust.

I wonder who sent him, she mused, bending down low under a canopy of trees. Adam? Old Mr Curlious?

"I will pray for you," Adam had said. God?

She sensed she was approaching a hamlet of some kind and she paused to ask a worker, hoeing a field of growing turnips, the name of the settlement ahead.

"Why, 'tis Fouracres, of course," he told her, glad to stop his job and indulge in a bit of idle chit-chat, "A strange, left-over place, much as you would leave the trimmings of fat meat on your plate and a smudge of gravy."

Verity shuddered.

I would not, she thought. No meat, fat or otherwise, would be on my plate.

"Do you know a lady by the name of Sarah White, by any chance?" she asked, "And I see you tend the land so have you, in your travels, come across a snake called the Davion?"

That made the elderly man prick up his ears.

"The Davion, eh?" he queried, "Why, I have not seen one of those since I was a boy. Wales's rarest snake, so my mother said. Just touching one with your hand could bring instant death. You steer clear of the Davion, Miss. But I doubt you'll find one were you to wander the length and breadth of Wales from North to South!"

On that pessimistic note, Verity wished him good day and made her way down the hill into the settlement which consisted of about twelve houses. Since the hoer did not know of a Sarah White, she asked the first person she saw, who was a tall, thin boy of about thirteen, bowling a hoop along.

"Miss White?" he murmured, "Ah, yes, she teaches us when we have a mind to go to school. A gentle soul, although I have been told she has a fiery temper if pushed. Rules the classroom with an iron rod but it has a velvet outer if you understand my meaning. I saw her leaning over her cottage gate not five minutes ago as I went past."

"Which house is hers?" asked Verity, thinking that they all looked alike apart from some niceties of colour.

"Why, the cherry pink one. Her wouldn't have the dark pink and said the pale one was almost red..."

Verity thanked the boy, who hovered about, evidently expecting a coin for his trouble, but soon concluded the woman was as poor as his teacher and sped off.

The cherry pink cottage was in the middle of the row and, on closer inspection, appeared the smallest but it was pretty too and well maintained. Huge hollyhocks were growing by the wall and a row of delphiniums clashed their blue against the pink dwelling. No one was in the garden so Verity opened the gate, timidly went up the path and knocked at the door. A dog barked from the interior and two black cats sprang onto the windowsill near her.

"Why, it's a real animal house," murmured Verity, forgetting about her task in stopping to stroke the cats. They purred loudly and arched their backs. It reminded her of Jet and she missed him so much that tears cascaded down from her lashes and dropped on to the path.

Coming to her senses, Verity realised the door had been opened and a small, birdlike woman was standing there watching her.

"Can I help you?" she asked at last, when she observed her visitor was aware of her presence.

"I do apologise," replied Verity, "I was charmed by your pair of cats and forgot my manners in their beauty."

The woman seemed pleased with Verity's praise of her felines and told her guest that they had both been saved from drowning by a cruel farmer because of their colour.

"I, too, have a small, black cat called Jet at home and he came to me as a stray, doubtless having been kicked or abused, judging by his fear. People are wicked in their treatment of animals, who cannot tell us the atrocities they have suffered at the hands of these tyrants. I would..." She tailed off, realising she was getting carried away and that the purpose of her coming was receding.

"I am sorry but it is a subject I feel very strongly about," she told her new companion.

"I, too, feel as you do, but I sense that is not the reason for your coming here?"

Verity shook her head.

"The cats were a diversion," she stated, "My real need is for your help, if you are Sarah White?"

"I am she," replied the woman.

"I heard you had studied the woodlands that belong to the Druid, Merlin, and that you may know the whereabouts of the Davion?"

Sarah was taken aback. No-one had mentioned the Davion for years it seemed, and now he stood alone, like a mythical creature in the Welsh heartlands, present but never seen, the stuff of folklore and witches' fables.

"Do you believe in magic?" she asked her guest and was again taken aback by the vigorous nod and positive affirmation she received.

"I would not be here if I did not," Verity told her.

It was an hour later and Verity sat on a well upholstered chair, fussing a little white terrier with one hand and the pair of black cats with the other, her tea cold and forgotten on the table in front of her. She had told her new friend as much of her tale as she believed Sarah needed to know, but she had left Andrew out of it as she felt too emotional concerning him to recount it.

"The Davion…the Davion…" Sarah was saying now, searching her shelves for a book to give her more information.

"I mentioned the name to an elderly hoer in a field not far from here and he said he had not seen one since his boyhood."

Sarah frowned.

"They are increasingly rare. Fifty years ago they were hunted for their beautiful skin and people thought their blood would cure everything from toothache to consumption but, of course, it was all nonsense. Ah…here it is!" she cried, pouncing on the book she needed. She began to flick through the pages and came to exactly what she was looking for. "The Davion," she announced, passing over the book to Verity, who was obliged to stop fussing the animals and look. She saw a long green snake with attractive diamond shaped panels in purple on its side and a long yellow streak behind the head.

"The diamonds are its warning," Sarah told her, "It has a deadly poison in its head and will not hesitate to use it. Many men have been killed from treading on one and dogs too have been poisoned for attempting to roll it over, for they say it has a foul smell to warn off predators."

"Have you seen one?" asked Verity, returning the book, "I mean recently. Would you know where there was a chance of finding one hereabouts?"

Sarah considered the questions.

"I have not seen one for a full ten years," she acknowledged, "My teaching and the cottage keep me busy, I must say, and I have not thought of the Davion…"

"And the name too…I do not like to say 'it' about a living creature. I thought it meant holy or angelic," Verity replied, thinking of Andrew.

"I think the Welsh labelled it so with a tongue-in-cheek attitude," replied Sarah, "The snake is supposed to be the most bad tempered in our land and will strike at anything that threatens it or it...sorry...he comes across. You do not have to tread on a Davion for him to strike. Just walk near him and once he can feel your vibrations he will bite you!"

Verity shrugged her shoulders.

How did she get a skin from him without succumbing to his poison?

It was a few hours later and the heat of the day was just abating. Verity had recovered from her walk and, refreshed and replete from a good luncheon, she accompanied Sarah to the surrounding fields where there was a possibility the Davion lived.

"I make no promises, mind," the teacher said "It is so many years since I looked for one but this is the sort of habitat they prefer. Evening is the time they slither out but the warmth of the day may entice them out early. How we kill the snake though I do not know..."

"Oh we don't, we can't," replied Verity quickly, "I need a skin, not a body! I read in your book that, in early autumn, they shed their skin and I will wait, if necessary, for that to happen."

Sarah was astonished.

"But your prize?" she cried, "Can you afford to wait that long? It may be coming towards the end of May but September is three months away!"

Verity shrugged.

"I cannot kill him or her," she told her new friend, "That is impossible. My prizes must only be won with compassion, and to surrender one life for another is wrong in so many ways. First though, we must find a Davion and I feel that will be a difficult task in itself."

They looked in bushes and scree, under trees and by river banks and soon, dusk made itself apparent in the sky and Sarah said they must come out later, when darkness covered the firmament, after a meal and a rest.

"For I am well into my fifties," she told Verity, "and not as young or supple as you."

They returned three hours later but the search was fruitless. The next day they returned but found nothing and finally,

Sarah said they must try another area which was marshier and maybe more to the Davion's liking. A week went by and not a glimpse, so they moved on to yet another terrain, drier and more sandy in soil and sheltered by a small copse.

Verity was beginning to lose heart. How much longer could they continue to wander, searching for the elusive needle in a haystack? Then, twelve days after beginning the search, they got a tantalising clue.

The day was very hot and June had come in with high temperatures and bright blue skies. The surrounding meadows were rich with grasses and the hay was coming along nicely. Several farm wagons passed the women as they frequented the criss cross roads and one elderly man, with a cracked clay pipe, offered them a lift on his trailer, which was empty.

"You need not be a-feared it is going to get your smart clothes leery with dirt," he told them, when they hesitated, "'Tis only bushels of last year's wheat as has been in there today and they had clean sacks."

It was a good three miles to Sarah's cottage and the hottest part of the day was ahead, so they accepted and the elderly man shouted to them as he drove his horses slowly onwards. "So what are you doing in these parts, you being the school teacher, Miss, and surely better suited behind a desk or with a group of children at your feet."

Sarah explained it was a holiday for the next week or so due to building work going on at the local school, which had already taken a month.

"Ah, I heard of that," replied the farm worker, "An expensive business for the squire."

Sarah agreed that it was.

"But it still don't explain what you are doing roaming here and looking into every nook and cranny of the land! You've been doing it a fair while, so I am told."

Sarah frowned. Fouracres was rife with gossip it seemed and the next hamlet, Llanfair, was no different.

"We are trying to find a rare snake," began Verity, thinking it was her fault there was this explaining to do.

"A snake, eh?" replied the man, whipping up the horses as they tried to grab a mouthful of wiry grass.
"The Davion actually," continued Verity, not approving of the use of a whip on the tired horses.
"You don't say!" The man stopped the wagon, jumped down and began rolling up his sleeve. Turning to the women, he showed them a diamond shaped wound in his forearm.
"Do you know what this is?" he asked them both.

Verity shook her head but Sarah answered immediately, "The Davion's bite!"

Verity looked with more interest.
"Did it hurt?" she said.
"Did it hurt?" exploded the man, "Why, I was lucky to escape with my life! Many have died from the Davion and many have been wounded for life or driven mad by the poison. Oh, I hollered alright, just like a baby and they all rushed round to see what the matter was..."
"Recently?" asked Sarah, "Or was it many years ago and you keep the scar?"
"Oh, I'll keep the scar alright," came the reply, "I'll go to my grave with that but, yes, recently, and only three months ago. Coming out of hibernation, or something the doctor said. Good job the squire called for him as I was half-mad with pain and a little brandy went very nicely to making it bearable. The rest of the bottle was even better over the next few days as I lay in my bed and sweated it out. Now, I may be no expert but one thing I DO know is, you ladies do not want to go anywhere near no Davion!"

Verity looked at Sarah and Sarah looked at Verity. Had they found the road to prize number four?

It was cooler the next day and the women returned to the area where they met the wagon and headed for the farm the man had worked upon when he was bitten. As they expected, they received no welcome from the bailiff there.
"You want permission to come onto the farm to find a snake with the most deadly poison in the whole of Wales?" he

roared in anger, "So then, what do you propose to do when or if you find it?"

"We only want a skin from him so we, or rather I, shall wait until he sheds it and then leave him in peace," Verity told him.

The man looked at her and, removing his hat, scratched his head.

"Never in all my days have I heard such nonsense!" he replied, "Why you must want your heads examining, the pair of you! And you the village school mistress too, Miss White!"

"Yes, I remember teaching you, Mr Stall, when you were half the size you are now."

"Don't get me wrong, Miss, I remember your kindness to my mother and it is that, and only that, which prevents me from setting the dogs on you now!"

"So you agree to us having a look around?" asked Verity, "Do you know where the attack took place?"

"Yes, at Two Acre Bottom in a field called Two Tones on account of the soil there."

"Could you point us in that direction then, please?"

"Not so fast, Miss. Miss White I know and can vouch for but you...well, you are no native of Wales and your accent I cannot place."

"I am Miss Whittle and from the northern moors of Scar's End," Verity told him.

"Ah...the North. I took some grain there once and they all talked gibberish and pretended they could not understand me. They understood me pretty well when I offered them the grain at an inflated price! Ha ha!"

Verity was getting impatient.

"Could we see the field today or not?" she repeated, "For we have walked a long way and are tired."

"I shall have to ask the farmer and he doesn't like strangers in his fields. Upsets the cattle and sheep."

"We promise not to go near the livestock," Sarah said, "My friend's need of the snakeskin is really life or death."

"It'll be death alright when she touches the Davion," mumbled the bailiff, but he went off to find the farmer and came back after a few minutes to say the farmer had given them permission but only for a short while.

"I am sorry you feel that way, but the bailiff says I am to accompany you," The young lad was firm in voice and carried a staff that rivalled Verity's in size. He introduced himself as the crow scarer and said he was better than any scarecrow.

"I never sleeps nor takes my eyes off the blackies," he boasted.

Verity saw it was the only way they were going to be allowed to search for the Davion and she gave up. It seemed Sarah knew his mother so she took the boy's attention and Verity was able to walk alone. It only took a short time to get to the field and Verity began to search among the stones and plants whilst Sarah and the young lad, Billy, talked.

"Did you see the snake, or were you here when the man got bitten?" asked Sarah, looking for clues.

"I was in the next field," replied Billy, "I came running as fast as I could and saw the thing slithering away into the undergrowth, just by the copse there," and he pointed.

Verity made for the spot at a brisk walk and Sarah and Billy followed at a slower pace. There were a few exposed roots and Verity began to search, conscious that the farmer said they could only be here a little while. She put her arm down into one burrow at the base of a huge oak tree and heard an angry voice float back up to her.

"Who disturbs the Davion in his midday sleep? Do you not know I have enough poison in my head to immobilise the hand that threatens me?"

Verity removed her arm suddenly and Billy, who saw her, ran forward and asked if she had been bitten.

"No," she said.

"But you think there is a snake in there?"

What could she say? Yes, and the Davion spoke to her?

"I...I don't know," she said, "I felt a movement."

Before she could stop him the boy began to dig with his stick and, in time, he exposed a small, cosy burrow and the Davion.

"Got him!" he yelled, in triumph. He raised his stick to begin battering the snake but Verity rushed forward and grabbed it, wrestling the implement from him and throwing it aside.

"NO!" she screamed, "You will not murder him! This has to be done with compassion or my mission is doomed! I will not let you kill him, even though that would give me the skin I need to save my beloved!"

Sarah had reached them by then and she got hold of Billy who was repeating, over and over again, that his order from the bailiff was to kill any snake found.

"I don't care if it is the Davion or not, the thing must die," the lad said with conviction.

"Leave it, Billy, please and let Verity take a look at the creature for a moment. Come to the side with me," Sarah ordered, dragging the boy away. He picked up his stick and scowled but followed Sarah and stood by her.

Verity had the space she needed. She knelt down by the stunned Davion, her back to Sarah and Billy and whispered, "Please, little snake, listen to me. I mean you no harm and tried to protect you from violence. The boy is ignorant and does not see with my eyes. I need your help and a skin, but not as a consequence of your death. I have heard that in autumn you shed that skin for another and I implore you to let me have it. Would you do that for me?"

The Davion blinked his eye.

"I am rare, I am beautiful," he said, "I must protect myself from the human race that seeks to destroy me. Yes, I bite, but only when I am threatened. How come you need my skin? And why then, when you could have got it for nothing, did you thrust the boy aside?"

"Nothing is ever achieved by murder and violence," Verity affirmed, "If you came with me now I could protect you and you could live in Sarah's garden until your skin is shed. If you stay on this farm I fear that one of the workers may kill you!"

"Hmm..." said the Davion, "I had to bite a man who trod on me and then they pursued me but I slithered away before they could club me. If I come with you will you release me in a garden and feed me worms and snails and everything else I require?"

"I will," replied Verity, "You have my word on that. When your skin is shed you will be free to go where you wish. However, there are cats and a dog in this garden and you must not bite them, for they are innocent like you."

"I will do my best," promised the Davion, "I nearly died a few minutes ago and I must thank you for saving me. I owe you something for your mercy. Scant pickings here and always noise, noise, noise. I crave peace."

"And you shall get it," Verity vowed. "Wait there whilst I get my friend and the lad to move on."

She turned round to the two of them and asked,

"Can you give me a minute to skin the snake, for he is dead after all?"

Billy stepped forward.

"Let me do it, for I have a knife on me," he said, but Verity refused.

"I need to make a call of nature too," she mentioned, "So I would be grateful if you both could go back to the gate and wait for me there."

Billy was a bit embarrassed at this and turned back with Sarah but Verity sensed her friend knew that it was all an excuse. When the two were out of earshot, she turned to the Davion and asked him if he would travel wrapped in her scarf in her bag.

"Yes," said the snake, "As long as the top is open for me to breathe and the journey is not too long."

"I will not make it a second longer than it has to be," Verity promised.

She sighed with relief. The Davion was hers and all she had to do now was wait.

CHAPTER TWELVE

"I wondered why you wished to leave the farm so quickly," said Sarah, when Verity told her what she had achieved. "How did you get the Davion into the bag without being bitten?"

Verity longed to tell her the magical truth but knew that was for her only, so she remarked she had used considerable stealth.

"And an element of luck must have come into it too!" she told her friend.

"Someone is watching over you," remarked Sarah, as they walked back to the cottage along the winding summer lanes.

Verity immediately thought of Andrew and turned her attention skywards to the zenith which was as blue as possible but nothing was visible apart from a few high clouds and the blazing sun. She felt vaguely guilty in duping the farmer into thinking she had killed and skinned the snake and so had hurried away before he asked to see her handiwork. She tried not to jolt the poor Davion too much but he was silent until they came to Sarah's garden and then they both set about making a comfortable pen for him with plenty of foliage and stones to hide under.

Sarah then hurried away to make some tea and Verity was able to open her bag and let the confused reptile out.

"It will not be for long, dear Davion," she said, "Once your skin is shed I will let you free and you may go where you wish."

"I suppose there is no danger of my head being bashed in here," replied the snake a little ungratefully.

"None at all," Verity assured him, "So you think it may take a few weeks to shed your skin?"

"Depends on the food," replied the Davion, artfully, "The more food the fatter I shall get and then the sooner my skin will shed and you may take the prize!"

"We shall ensure you have a never-ending supply!" Verity told him, although she disliked giving live prey to captive animals, but it was the same with Jet. She just had to do as much as she could to prevent suffering.

For a few days Sarah and Verity were glad to rest, as the heat was high, and June passed without an incident. Meanwhile, the Davion grumbled but grew fatter and fatter.

Verity read Adam's parchment again and again and worried over the delay to take prize number four but she did not feel like calling up the black raven for a message. "They will view it as if I have had to give up or worse still, that I have died trying," she told herself a hundred times a day, "Then they may take what is left of Frederick to heaven's gates with good reason. Yet I need to tell them I am delayed but have won the first three prizes and now await the colours of autumn for the fourth. How shall I do that?"

She pondered and pondered and decided, in the end, to call up the black raven and see what he said. After all, she did not have to send him. Sarah was giving tuition to some young boys in the village who were behind with their work at school and so Verity took the opportunity to ascend to her bedroom, open the window and chant the rhyme –

"I need your help, bird of the air,
My soul is heavy, I must share,
Delay or worse has followed me
The path is dim, I cannot see
The next stage of my journey, so
I remain here and cannot go
A messenger I am allowed
To take my words, I am not proud
I did my best, I need your wings
To take my letter of these things,
Fly straight and quick – you must depart
And bring some hope to this sad heart."

No sooner had she finished this chant, when she heard a beating of wings in the air and a large, black raven landed on the open window, almost beside her.

"Greetings!" he said, cocking his head and winking one eye, "You do not seem dead so I suppose delay haunts your path and blocks it?"

"True, my friend, it does," Verity replied to him, "So tell me what I do? Do I send you, and then Adam fears my death and Lawrence stakes my beloved, or do I just wait and hope they understand?"

"I am the bird of bad news, the bird of ill omen and death and disaster," replied the raven, "But there is a way open to you, should you wish to take it. A message you are allowed if your path is closed or diverted, as I suppose it is. However, it will not be me."

"Then who?" asked Verity, "For the Davion may need another month or more to shed his skin and as I wait, Frederick could be sent to heaven...or hell," she added as an afterthought.

"My friend the pigeon will go for you," replied the raven, "He carries a neutral vibration and you have already used the ouzel bird. True, he is not white but he is not black either. I will call him for you," and he emitted a shrill shriek.

From out of nowhere, a large plum and white pigeon arrived and preened his wings as he sat next to the raven on the windowsill.

Verity was a little confused.

"You will take my message then?" she asked the new arrival.

"So it seems," replied the pigeon, "Do you have it ready, as I tuck my head under my wings once nine o'clock has rung and gone?"

Verity shook her head.

"Not yet," she admitted, "But I can write a note in a few minutes and give it to you. I know where Sarah keeps her paper and she has a pen and ink downstairs."

"Very well," cooed the bird, "I shall nap on this ledge and my friend had better be off to collect his peck of bad tidings. I bring neither joy nor tragedy. A delay I suppose on your journey?"

"Yes," replied Verity, but the pigeon had tucked his head under his wing and gone to sleep and a whirr of wings announced the departure of the raven.

"I hope this letter finds you well, Adam, and that it finds Frederick still undead and not yet seated at Abraham's bosom. I am sure I would have known in my heart if Lawrence had staked him but I realise it must be such a struggle for him, and for you too.
Adam, I have succeeded in winning the first three prizes, and they are safely put away for the Green Witch, but the fourth one delays me by a month or two. So, my journey may be longer and harder and the time I shall spend away from you could now amount to half a year. Well, what is that? In the eyes of God and the realms of eternity it is nothing but I am well and I am still determined to reach the end of this stony road and claim my beloved back.
Give all my love to Lawrence and a small portion to Frederick. I dream of him when I sleep but it is the old Frederick, who worked so hard to eradicate the vampires at Scar's End. Could it be a premonition? Could it be the world telling me to wait and that man will walk back into my life? I hope it is so.
I will see you before the winter turns the land white and I will be the victor. I hope and pray the ouzel bird is well and happy with you.
Your loving
Verity."

She folded up the letter and sighed. I am writing of a confidence I do not feel, she thought. Whether Adam would see through it, she did not know, but she had to emit a wave of achievement to keep Lawrence on side. How difficult had Frederick been since she left, she wondered? For so long she had put him out of her mind but he came to her then, pleading and begging on his knees.
"Leave this, my darling, leave this and come home to me! I need you! I need you!"

She shook her head to dispel the image and sent him just a little of her love.

"I will be with you soon enough, my angel, but my task is not completed and when it is, I shall transform you into your former glory!" She felt him shudder at her emotion and she left him and returned to the messenger.

Fastening the letter gently to his wing she fed the pigeon some corn that Sarah often put out for the birds when the cats were in and softly snoring.

"Fly straight...fly true, my dear friend and take my missive, so they know I am safe but not yet ready to return to the monastery!"

The pigeon stretched his wings after his sleep, uttered a cry of goodbye, and took off into the sky. She watched him grow smaller and smaller and then, although she leant from the window, he was gone.

The next day, about midday, Adam was working in the garden and gathering the vegetables needed for lunch when he heard a coo, and a pigeon, obviously exhausted and spent, landed at his feet. He picked the bird up and immediately knew this pigeon had more to tell him.

Carrying the bird to a warm spot, he fetched water and corn together with split peas and watched the tired pigeon feed. Then, to his amazement, the bird spoke to him.

"I carry a message from Verity Whittle. She would not send the black raven as that would indicate failure and she has not failed. She merely waits to claim the fourth prize. Once I have handed over her letter, I will become what I was before the magic summoned me – a plum and white pigeon."

Looking at his new friend more closely, Adam could see a sheet of paper was folded small and fastened loosely to the underside of the bird's wing. He removed it carefully and opened Verity's missive.

After reading the short message twice, he smiled with relief that Verity was still alive and doing well, if her confidence was to be believed.

"About to claim the fourth prize!" he told the pigeon but, although the bird blinked a knowing eye at him, Adam knew the magic had fled and the bird was just a pigeon.
"You are beautiful nevertheless," he told the messenger, "You shall come rest in the dovecote and live with the others there, if you so choose. Bless you tiny friend, for bringing us the good news safely from wherever Verity struggles. The fourth prize within her grasp is good but the fifth prize will take every scrap of energy she has left!" His face became pensive as he remembered the road he had travelled not that long ago and he sent her love and luck. Picking up the pigeon, he took him to the dovecote and found him a peaceful perch in the large, white home.

Later, after lunch was finished, he sought Lawrence who was just waking up and he told him the good news.
"Is it?" replied that gentleman, irritably. "More months away and Frederick getting harder and harder to deal with every day!"
"I help when I can," replied Adam, annoyed at Lawrence's negative words, "She is more than half way through her challenges and by winter, or before, she will be on her way back here."
Lawrence sighed.
"You believe this fable," he told Adam, "but I do not. Despite what the Reverend Father told me, I have doubts and am very sceptical. Time will tell I suppose and I will do as you and she ask and give her a few more months but a year, no."

Adam could only hope that the dragon was amiable and that the Green Witch was able to give Verity exactly what she needed to free her love's heart from the box of doom.

Summer waned and the evenings drew in, so that Verity and Sarah were obliged to light the candles a great deal earlier. The Davion was growing fatter and fatter and Verity was sure she had seen a small tear in his green skin, just where the diamonds bordered his head. She told Sarah this as they sat before the first fire of the season, nursing cats and the dog on their laps, with Sarah knitting Verity a warm jumper to take with her when she left.

"It is the first of September tomorrow," Sarah said, "I still have a sleeve to do so you must not leave me yet, dear friend."

Verity smiled.

"I am at the Davion's beck and call," she replied, "However, I am sure I saw that small gap and he knew I did, too."

"You are giving human attributes to a reptile," Sarah laughed.

"Oh, it is merely the magic of my quest," Verity told her, "I am sure I will wake up very soon and find the Davion possessed of a fine new skin."

Sarah measured out the sleeve she was finishing and said that another few rows would see her able to sew the garment together.

"For even if you leave tomorrow," she said, "Darker days are in front of you and I fear the final prize will be the hardest to attain."

Verity was sure of that. Later, she went to bed and leant out of her bedroom window, feeling the night breeze lift her hair and cool her worried brow. Still so much to do…

She slept fretfully and a picture of Frederick came to her, Frederick on his knees begging for his life…could it be that the pigeon had not arrived and given Adam her note, she worried?

"Spare me, save me, help me, Verity. They plan to take my life and the gates of heaven swing wide open but, equally, the fires of hell burn bright for me…Leave your quest and come to me…It has been far too long…too long…"

Verity was steadfast though and she knew this was another trick by the vampires to put her off her scent.

"Not long now," she sent back, "Just one more prize and the witch will help me convince the dragon to release your heart…"

"But you can do that with just one bite…an exchange of our blood…we do not need another. My heart is given to the

creatures of night and they crave yours too! Give it up and come to me!"
"No, no!" she sent back, "I love you too much to do that. Do you hear me? I love you!"

She felt him wince and draw off. Dawn was coming, gentle and fragrant with birdsong and red skies. She got up and there, in the garden, was the sight she needed to complete this stage of her task.

The Davion had shed his skin.

"I really cannot stay another day," Verity told her friend later that day, when the skin had been cleaned, admired and wrapped up in Verity's luggage, "Speed is of the essence now and the last great task beckons..."

Had she not read the final verse once the Davion had given up his precious skin and emerged, whole and happy, in a brand new coat?

"The final prize, it must be won
Whether the skies bring rain or sun,
The final leg it lies before
To open up the witches door,
She waits for you, for prizes five
So keep your hopes of life alive.
Your last task is the biggest one,
This animal, it weighs a ton
And deep in folklore he'll arise
To capture him you must be wise
Be cunning, brave, and seize the day
Because there is no other way.
So what, you ask, will I reveal
The creature of the golden seal
Search the woods from dawn to dusk
You need some of the golden tusk…
A fragment or a chunk will do
But will this huge boar come for you?
He has killed many in his rage
So capture him and turn the page!"

Turn the page, thought Verity, and what do I find on the other side? She felt suddenly afraid…a boar, of monstrous proportions, with golden tusks! Where did she find him? She went to thank the Davion and to say goodbye.

"Dear Davion – I must leave you and, as I release you from the run, I thank you for your kindness in giving me the part of you that you have shed. I trust your new skin is better for you?"

The Davion blinked his wise eye.

"A little snug at the moment and a little stiff but I shall snuggle my way into it and enjoy the thicker skin I have grown. You are welcome to my cast-off and, before you go, I must do you whatever favour you require before my magical powers flit and fade. Autumn is in the air. I smell it, even though my nostrils, as such, are closed. I will gladly stay in this excellent run and use its protection against the winter storms, which are surely on the way. What is your wish, my lady? You waited for me and showed me compassion so I must do the same."

Verity thought hard.

"My last prize is the hardest of all, brave Davion, as I have to find the boar with the golden tusks. Have you heard of him and could you tell me where to find him?"

The snake cocked his head to one side.

"Ah, you speak of Garth the Great, feared by all who come across him! Why the ground shakes when he walks and the trees bow down to him! He paws the earth and charges at the quaking men who follow him. His huge golden tusks have tossed and impaled many a Welshman on his innocent journey. You will struggle with him, Verity, and you will need help if you are to gain even a fragment of his tusk. Many is the man who has set out on a fierce stallion to spear him but the warrior has never been seen again. I can do little against such power..."

"But you know where he lives?" asked Verity, feeling fear creep over her, "My verse gives me no clue as to where, in all of Wales, he lives."

"Yes, I can point out the very forest where he hunts and has his lairs. However, there is an easier way for you to get there. Do you leave today?"
"I had thought to, before darkness covers the land as it is September now and eight o'clock sees dusk descending."
"Come to me when you are ready to leave and I will summon up the winged horse to take you to Garth's door!"

Verity went to say her goodbyes to Sarah and to thank her for her hospitality and help in tracking down the Davion. The two women hugged and then Verity shouldered her bag, took her staff in her hand and went out into the garden to see if the Davion had kept his word.

There, in the meadow behind the house, was a magnificent grey horse with huge white wings and a saddle made of gold. Verity could hardly believe her eyes. The horse neighed and plunged up and down but when Verity mounted him, he quietened down and, spreading his wings of white feathers, he soared into the sky. Up and up he went into the ether and Verity hung on tight, barely able to look down. The clouds were so near she could touch them and the air was full of sparkling raindrops. She saw a rainbow in the distance and fixed her eyes upon it. Was it a lucky omen for her and Frederick?

The horse soared over cottages, hamlets and fields and with every beat of his powerful wings, Verity felt the last prize was getting nearer and nearer.

"Goodbye, dear Davion!" she called, and a blur of green beneath her swept up and faded. She was on her way to challenge Garth, the wild boar, and to convince him, with compassion, to shed her a fragment of his tusk.

CHAPTER THIRTEEN

The air was blue with cold, despite the warm summer afternoon, so high did they fly and the clouds were within arm's reach.

Pure, bracing gossamer, thought Verity. So it is when we walk through mist and the air is heavy with moisture. It was as though rain had fallen but her clothes were dry and the precious cargo that she carried.

Dear Frederick, she thought, I face the greatest challenge of my life and all for you...all for you. How I miss you... Again his voice came into her head but she shook her long, dark hair and banished him. Now was not the time to ponder on love as she had to keep alert and her hands clung onto the horse's plentiful mane.

She felt they were descending and into her head came the Davion's voice,
"I have done my best for you, Verity, as you did your best for me. We are released from obligation to each other and I bless you in your journey. Good luck!"

Back came the reply from her heart.
"Long and happy life, Davion, for now you will truly become what you were when I first beheld you, a snake, but always precious, because you shed your skin for me!" She sensed he had already lost the magic and her attention was then upon the nearness of the ground as they descended into what appeared to be a forest clearing.

The horse's silver hooves hit the earth and he circled and stopped, so Verity was able to get off and remove her bag and staff from his back. Before she could say a word, he had flapped those giant wings and set off, once more, for the skies. She watched him get smaller and smaller and suddenly the sky was empty.

She looked around her. Tall trees on all sides but a plentiful supply of long grass on the forest floor and an earth mound to her left which the horse had landed on. Nothing seemed visible and there was no sound.

She began to walk on, feeling an eerie wind wandering around her and tugging at her cloak and hair. A mile or more later the forest still surrounded her and she had seen no signs of life. Then, suddenly, to her right, she heard voices. Men! Two, maybe three of them! At first they spoke in Welsh and she had no idea what they said but then another joined the group and she heard them change to English.

"And why should we succeed when so many other men have failed?" said one, "What do we possess that others do not? It seems a fool's game to me and one calculated to rob us of our lives."

"He has to be caught," replied another, "Why, he mauled a man and his horse only a few days ago and impaled the poor beast to a tree, then he went back for the rider."

"I agree he must be caught but why should it be us risking all?" a third declared.

"Are we not the youngest and strongest warriors in the village?" the first declared, "If not us, then who? Our wives and children are frightened to search the woodlands for spring flowers, summer fruits and autumn mushrooms. How many years is he going to reign here and frighten us all?"

"So how do you propose to bring him down?" the second man asked, "We have tried bow and arrows and they just glance off him. Poison he will not touch and dogs he kills with a single blow. Yet he carries in his head a hundred pounds of gold and we could claim that and make ourselves a small fortune!"

"What use is that if we are dead? Or do you propose to give that to our wives by means of compensation when he has mangled us?" the third asked.

Verity stood very still listening and wondered what they could be talking of but it seemed likely to be of Garth. She had hidden herself behind a tree and she was glad she had done so when the ground seemed to shake and into the woodland glade thundered the very animal himself. She heard the men exclaim and make a dash for their horses but the animal pawed the ground and uttered a great cry before fleeing off in the opposite direction. The men had no time to mount before the creature was gone and they bewailed the fact that an opportunity had been missed.

"Never was there a greater chance to capture him and us too slow to follow!" they cried.

To Verity, the boar had been nothing more than an upset animal and one, she sensed, who was in pain. The cry was one of anguish, not of genuine ill temper, and she proposed to wait for the men to go and then follow Garth's tracks. The fact that it was highly dangerous never occurred to her. Humans were dangerous and cruel too, but animals were only frightened and needed help. She crouched down as the three men on horseback passed her hiding place and then, when the noise of their passing had receded, she left her cover and followed in the wake of the giant boar.

She walked for over an hour and saw nothing, apart from a few squirrels climbing the trees and a number of small birds picking over bits on the forest floor. Once a woodpecker startled her by loud drumming against the trunk of an oak but apart from that, all was still.

Eerily still, she thought. It is as though everything has vanished from the face of the earth and I am the only human being left. Her anxiety rose a little.

The sun was beginning to wane in the sky and she knew evening was near, and the unpleasant reality of spending a night in the forest loomed large in her mind. She wondered where the boar had gone to ground and what it was that pained him and had caused that cry of anguish? She feared the men would succeed and either shoot or spear him if he became any worse.

Then, just as she rounded an overgrown thicket of bramble, she saw Garth ahead of her, pawing the ground and snorting in fury. A few feet away from him, two men took aim with bow and arrow. Verity was furious and, not thinking of her own safety, she rushed forward and pushed the bowman's hand, just as he was going to shoot. His arm shot skywards and the arrow went up and lodged in the branch of an overhanging tree.

Meanwhile, the giant boar had taken the scene in and used it to bolt off, leaving a furious archer and his friend glaring at Verity. She got in first.

"That is not the way!" she cried angrily, "You have no right to murder him! Can you not see he is sick and in pain? That is why he behaves as he does! Why are you too blind to see it?"

Faced with such passion the men were taken aback.

"He has killed many of our chickens when he rampages through the village and he has gored numerous men and horses sent to dispatch him," said the bowman, retrieving his arrow and returning it to the quiver on his back.

"You have no right to 'dispatch him', as you call it. If you were in pain, and no one helped you, would you want to be dispatched with an arrow?"

The other man stepped forward and told her to mind her own business.

"The treatment of animals is my business, it is everybody's business," Verity told him, "He feels every emotion you and I do and he feels pain too. Why, I bet I could discover why he behaves as he does and take steps to ensure he never goes on the rampage again!"

The archer shrugged his shoulder.

"Brave words but he would gore you to pieces in a moment were you to try!"

"I think not," Verity assured him, "I am game enough to attempt it and, in fact, need to, in order to discover exactly what is wrong with him!"

"Ho ho," laughed the second man, "You think you can put it right then?"

"Yes," Verity told him confidently, "If I cannot, I will find someone who can, that I do know, and there will be no putting an arrow in him, for sure."

The two men looked at each other.

"Very well," said the archer, "Shake on it and we promise not to kill the boar if you can sort out his unpredictable behaviour but if you lose, we can spear him and enjoy his carcass roast on a spit!"

Verity shuddered. Heaven forbid, she thought.

She hesitantly put out her hand and shook with both but she noticed her fingers were shaking. For good or for ill, she had taken on a massive challenge that, if she got it wrong, could cost her her life.

Within a few minutes Verity found herself alone in the woodland glade and darkness coming down fast. The dusk was suddenly chill and she realised this was the biggest hill she had ever had to climb in her life. She found a somewhat sheltered spot near the bole of a giant tree and, grateful for the presence of the spreading giant, she pulled her cloak around her and hugged her knees to her chin.
If Garth decided to charge her now… She heard footsteps coming through the forest and fear caused her to duck down out of sight in case the men were back and bent on revenge for her earlier actions.
How could you have issued such a challenge, her head said. You do not know these men nor what they are capable of. You are a sitting target here.

Fear gripped her as she peered out from the trunk but it was a small, fair woman walking towards her carrying a bundle of what looked like blankets and she had a bag over her arm, too. She turned her head this way and that as if looking for someone and when she drew level with the tree she cried out,
"Hello! Hello! I come to bring you food and warmth, for the night may be chill and my husband, fool that he is, told me of your declaration! I release you from it now! He would never put a life in danger! Hello! Hello!"

The fear left Verity's heart and she stood up and stepped forward.
"Your husband does not need to do that," she told the woman, "I meant every word I said."

The wife threw down her bundle and began to unpack her bag too, bringing forth bread and a flagon of water together with some meat, which Verity grimaced at.

"I thank you for your kindness," she said, conscious she was being rude, "However, I do mean to help the giant boar, and not for monetary gain either. I help him because he is a sentient creature who is obviously in pain."

The blonde woman invited Verity to sit and eat with her but, seeing Verity's expression when she tried to pass her the meat, she asked what ailed the food.

"It was once a living, breathing animal," Verity told her, "The poor creature has been killed for that pathetic lump of rotting flesh and I will not be part of this murder! I shall do very nicely with the bread, thank you."

The woman introduced herself.

"I am Marion," she told Verity, "I am the wife of Gareth, the younger man you spoke to. He meant no harm by his words but you took him by surprise, and his older brother, Owain, too. They came straight home to me and I told them that no lady should be left alone in the wood at night whilst Garth wanders..."

"I am not afraid of the boar..." began Verity, but Marion interrupted her.

"Then you should be. There are tales of him goring sleepers in the woods and killing their horses too."

"You have seen that with your own eyes?" asked Verity.

"No, but there are many stories like that circulating round the village. The boar must be killed before he causes any more deaths."

"So, you are not prepared to give me a chance to prove it is only pain that drives Garth to behave as he does?"

Marion looked at her feet.

"I would rather you did not risk your life," she replied quietly, "My husband feels the same, so we exonerate you from your promise and ask that you go on your way safely at first light tomorrow and leave us to deal with the boar."

Verity was very angry.

"I made a promise," she said, "I shook on it, so it is now my word and my bond. However, I would be grateful for your presence on the morrow when we track Garth down, as I believe I can help him. I need something from him too, and I

think, as I have done in the past, I can trade compassion for a life."
"You are determined to stay and track the boar down then?" asked Marion, rising to her feet when it was apparent that Verity was going to eat no more.
"Yes," replied Verity, trying to feel confident about the morrow, "I do thank you, though, for your kindness and if you leave everything but the meat, I shall enjoy it for my breakfast."

Marion nodded.

"You are as stubborn as I am, I see," she smiled, "Of course, keep the food, as there are the last of our summer fruits in that bag and apples too, which have been wrapped in paper and stored in our attic. I can bring you some fresh bread in the morning and more water too."

"Thank you," Verity told her, "I know you may not understand me but I have to do it, as more than Garth's life rests on this. I am on a strange journey and after this confrontation, if it goes well, I am near the end and I am very weary."

"I shall leave you to sleep then," replied Marion, "I shall come and find you in the morning and I shall pray you have a peaceful night."

Verity thanked her again and felt, in her heart of hearts, Marion understood that so much was at stake for her. She had to acquire the last prize or there was no future for her and Frederick.

It was a few hours later and Verity had managed to get herself comfortable and warm within the blankets, which she was glad were of woven cloth and not wool, and the woodland seemed at peace. It had been a long day and she was conscious that tomorrow, she faced a life or death situation. Her head ached with exhaustion so she lay down and kind sleep blew gently over her dark hair and closed, weary eyes…

She did not see, drifting down from the air and the tall, silent trees, a huge cloak composed of blue and silver. It fell about her shoulders but did not disturb her, and it swirled around her feet so she was encased in its magic. Its owner gazed down at her, shook his feathery wings and smiled at the sweetness of her sleep.

Bending down, he allowed his lips to graze her cheek and feel the ivory smoothness of her face.

"Rest well, brave warrior!" he whispered but Verity did not stir. Taking up guard over his precious charge, the angel folded his wings and let his eyes search the darkness. Nothing would come near her that night.

It was broad daylight when Verity awoke and the woodland was filled with a cold mist that swirled around the trees and played games in the leafy bowers. Autumn was on its way. She could taste it in the air and feel it in the keen breeze that greeted the dawn of day. She shivered…

An hour later, she had washed in a cold stream and was eating the remains of the bread and fruit which Marion had brought her last night.

Would they find the giant boar today, she worried, and more to the point, would he attack her? She pictured herself crushed and bruised, with broken bones and bloodied face and hands. How could she continue her quest then?

About mid morning, Marion returned with her husband and another man, who she introduced as her brother. They carried ropes and the brother had a primitive gun slung over his arm. Verity was unnerved.

"Why have you got that?" she asked, when introductions were over and they started off on their hunt for Garth.

"Do not fear, Miss," replied Bryn, Marion's brother, "I am no archer like Owain but I am a fair shot with this gun once I have loaded it with gunpowder."

"But I said there was to be no bloodshed," Verity affirmed.

"If the giant boar has you impaled on his tusks we will have to shoot him so as to release you," replied Marion, calmly, "We cannot leave you to your fate."

"That will not happen," Verity told her, "I mean to ascertain exactly what troubles Garth and causes him the pain he is in."

"So you still do not believe his general bad temper is down to the fact he is a wild animal?"

Verity shook her head.

"There is more to it, I am sure," she told her audience, "I mean to help the boar, not kill or maim him. No matter what, I do not want you to kill him. I want your word on that if we find him."

The two men looked at each other and shrugged.

"If that is what the lady wants..." began Gareth.

"She does. In fact she insists on it as part of the deal we shook on."

Reluctantly they agreed and Marion took the gun. Verity could see she doubted the brave words uttered and thought Verity mad to put her faith in such a dangerous animal.

Closing her eyes, Verity prayed that she was right and that Garth recognised the fact that she wished to help him.

"Dear God, make him aware that I come in peace and with the intention of ending the pain he is in," she muttered under her breath.

The little party moved on.

It was nearly dusk when they found evidence the great boar was near. They were all tired and hot and thirsty too, despite bringing water and food.

Bryn found a small lock of the animal's hair where he had rubbed himself against a tree.

"He must be close now," he said and it sent a shiver of mingled excitement and fear down Verity's spine. She began to send out gentle thoughts.

Garth, Garth, I know you are in pain. I come in peace and though the men around me carry ropes and there is a gun, it is not meant for you. Garth, Garth, I come to help you...

Back through the trees came a jumble of words and emotion...

I do not believe you. Men come with bows and arrows to kill me, and for what? My golden tusks, my fine coat, my tender flesh...how can you be any different to those you travel with? What company you keep...Murderers...

Yes, yes, but I want to prove to them there is nothing to be gained by killing you. I want to cure you. Tell me where it hurts. Tell me.

"I think I saw him through yonder trees," cried Gareth.

Verity's heart was racing but she repeated, over and over again.

I come in peace, I come to help you, let me help you!

Back came the answer

No, no, you want my life, you want my tusks...

No, just a fragment to save the life of him I love. First, though, I want to cure you. I want to end your pain...

Suddenly, they all saw him in a small clearing up ahead. "Please draw back all of you," Verity told the three, "He does not trust you. He fears you. Please move aside and let me speak to him."

Surprisingly the three did as asked and waited in the shelter of a tall tree. Verity moved forward. She was shaking with fear but she knew she must exhibit confidence and, above all, compassion.

"Garth! Garth!" she called, realising he was but twelve feet away, "I come to help you. See, I have no weapons to destroy you and I am alone. My friends have gone!"

The boar moved a little closer. His reply came back after a couple of minutes but only Verity heard it. To the others the air was silent.

"I do not believe you. I have been hunted for many months now and why should you be any different?"

"I can help you, Garth! We do not have to be enemies!"

The boar pawed the ground again and shook his head.

"You smell of fear and you smell of death. I do not trust you!" he sent back and suddenly, he was charging towards her. Verity stood her ground and, feeling the solidarity of the staff in her hand, she rubbed the tiger's face and whispered,

"Help me now...please...Old Mr Curlious said you could if I am in mortal danger," She rubbed and rubbed and Garth was almost in slow motion, so that it appeared time had stopped and his eyes changed from emitting anger to complete surprise.

A massive tiger leapt from the staff and lifted his enormous paws up in the air as he protected Verity with his striped body. She gasped and Garth stopped dead in his tracks.

"I talk to you, animal to animal," cried the tiger, swishing his tail and drawing himself up to full height, "Respect me, wild Garth, for I have your best interests at heart. You and I share the same blood, the same heart, the same soul. Humans have trapped and killed many of us. Imprisoned us to perform acts to entertain humanity when they are bored or need excitement. They have used our bones and glands for so-called cures from their diseases and they hunt and shoot us for sport. This woman is not one of these. She comes in peace and to help you. Her arms are open to you, as is her heart. She wants to help you. Her beloved lies in the grasp of a vampire and only by obtaining a tiny piece of one of your golden tusks can she restore him to her life. Help her, brave Garth, and she will help you."

The talk was interrupted by a shot that, luckily, went over the head of the giant boar and Verity knew one of the men had fired the weapon. They had lied to her.

"Quick, quick, Garth – we must fly!" she cried and in an instant, she was on his back and they were galloping through the forest and away from the sound of gunshot, death and broken promises. Verity held on to Garth's luxurious mane and looked down at the staff, now tucked under her arm. Did her tired eyes really betray her, for she could have sworn that the tiger was smiling...

On and on they raced and Verity felt the cool air rushing past her face as the trees began to thin out and they came to the edge of the forest. Suddenly Garth swerved to avoid a deep bog and Verity lost hold of his mane and flew through the air, landing, fortunately, on some dry grass. She was winded for a moment and the bag on her back had jarred her spine considerably in the fall. She lay there for a minute, recovering, and wondered if Garth would leave her. She called his name.

"I am here," he replied, "Are you hurt?"

"No, only winded," she said, trying to get up and restoring her bag. Her staff lay at her feet and...what was that? Out of the side of her eye, she could have sworn she saw the flicker of angel wings...Andrew!

The boar stood quiet now, blowing a little, and Verity approached him and ran her hand along his body.

"Tell me where it hurts," she said.

Garth flung his head up and opened his mouth, so that Verity could see a massive abscess on one tooth and that tooth black and rotten.

"I knew it!" she cried, "I knew you were in pain! I could sense it the time you ran through the forest away from us!"

The boar's eyes were misty.

"I can barely eat or sleep," he said, "In vain do I bang my head against trees and walls to get rid of the tooth that is causing my anguish. By night, I feel feverish and hot, by day, cold and weak and yet still the men hunt me."

Verity was searching the grass and the boggy ground for the plants she needed to make a length of string and eventually she found them, twining together, and began to pull them apart.

After a few minutes she had made a length of twine that was strong and she then approached the boar and told him to trust her.

"This may hurt at first, Garth, but believe the words of the tiger if you do not believe me. I need to get your rotten tooth out before it poisons your whole system. I can tie this around your tooth and then attach it to the nearest tree, so you must pull against it and the molar will come clean from your jaw. Do you trust me? Can I put this in your mouth?"

Garth nodded.

"I sense you only want good things for me," he said, "I shall do as you ask," and he obediently opened his mouth.

The twine was fixed and Verity tied the end to a tree and asked the boar if he was ready to run. He nodded, half mad with the pain from the infection. Verity waited a minute then counted down…
"Three, two, one..."

She gave him a slap on his rump and he took off, the twine pulling against him and, suddenly, the tooth was out and lying black and bloodied on the grass. Verity breathed a sigh of relief.

It was an hour later and Verity had found a stream and bathed and bathed Garth's mouth with the pure water. The boar was already feeling better and he lowered his head and nuzzled her gratefully. As he did so, Verity noticed a small fragment of his left golden tusk was missing.
"Garth! You have lost a portion of your tusk! Do you know where? It is as the tiger said, I need a small piece of it to save my beloved! Did you lose it today, for we cannot go back to the forest as it will be too dangerous?"
"No, no, I do not think I lost it there," replied the boar, "I tried to sleep here and the pain tormented me so that I banged my head against the field wall over there. I may have dislodged it then."

Verity looked over to a dry stone wall that divided the marshy ground they presently stood on, from an area of grassland where sheep grazed. In an instant she had run over there and began searching the ground for anything bright and shiny.

Wandering up and down, she thought her luck was out but, upon raising her eyes, she saw a shining fragment of gold on one of the stones that jutted out from the wall and she seized it triumphantly. It was her last, precious prize.

CHAPTER FOURTEEN

"You showed me compassion and, for that, I am obliged to do you a favour before the magic fades and I become a wild boar again."

It was four hours later, both Verity and Garth had slept and whilst they rested, the indigo tones of an autumn evening smudged their colours in the sky. Darkness was approaching but Verity was anxious to get her five prizes to the Green Witch before any more demons came to plague her. She thought long and hard about the favour whilst reading the last verse on Adam's parchment -

Five prizes sit square in your hand
But move them and they slip like sand;
The witch is waiting, steeped in green
The dragon calls, his heart is mean
He'll give so little love away
So seize the jewels and save the day.
Where, now, you ask, does this witch live
And for my prizes will she give
The sapphires and the rubies red
That end the sleep and wake the dead?
Search over land, through wood and dell
But listen – hark – she spins a spell
Her voice is high, her words profound
Creep up and do not make a sound
Put the five prizes to the test
And you become the witch's guest
She's waited for the beauty rare
So rest awhile, draw up a chair,
The spirits of the air wear smiles,
Your journey has a few more miles
Take to the dragon sparkling parts
And then exchange them for a heart…

"Do you know where the Green Witch lives?" Verity asked the boar, "Could you take me there before darkness descends?"

Garth stretched and yawned.

"I could," he said, "She lives at Withy End only a mile from here. Climb upon my broad back and we shall fly! A mile is a mere step for me and we can be there in a few minutes with my speed. My fear now is to come back to this land and be hunted again and speared. What must I do to protect myself?"

Verity climbed onto his back and said she would consult the witch as to his best course of action.

"For I want to ask her for some hypericum for your mouth and you need somewhere to lay your head whilst you heal. She must be the witch of all the witches in this area so, as such, she should know of a sanctuary where hunters are kept away. I am conscious that once you have done this for me you will be a boar again but I have no doubts that your ferocity will disappear and your gentleness will return."

The stars were becoming visible in the sky, so they flew and the land was eaten up in Garth's rapid strides. A small village was reached and they clattered past onto a lonely common.

"This is Withy End," Garth told her, "Our journey is nearly over. The fourth cottage on the left is Greenlands and there the witch resides. Does she expect you?"

Verity dismounted and walked the last few paces.

"I think not," she said, "However, she knows what I bring adds up to a pile of jewels which I understand she can bring forth from the prizes I have in my bag."

Garth laughed.

"It has long been said that she is not very good at spells," he retorted, leaving Verity a little worried.

They found the cottage with the sign Greenlands and a candle burnt in the window so Verity knocked loudly, once, twice, thrice and at last a head appeared from an upstairs window and a voice shouted down,

"Who is there? Have you lost your horse and wish me to find it or have you misplaced your spectacles? Yes, I have a spell for that, if I could remember it."

A mane of black hair appeared and the witch scratched her head.

"Ah, you have a boar. Is it he or she you are wishing to magic away?"

"No," called Verity, "He needs your help, it is true, but I wish you to do a spell on my behalf and I have brought all the rare things you need to perform it."

"A spell?" cried the witch, in delight. "Why, you have come to the right place! I would come down and let you in but I have mislaid the back door key and am attempting to perform a ritual to find it. Now, where was I? Oh yes, a pinch of dust, well there is plenty of that here, and a pinch of earth...I think I have a potted plant somewhere..."

She shut the window with a bang and Verity heard her muttering whilst the boar laughed.

"It seems she has not changed," he said, "You must perform your own spell, I'll be bound. If you could get in that is."

However, the ritual must have worked as Verity heard the back door being unlocked and opened and they both hurried round there.

"Ah! Freedom at last!" said the witch, who did not look like a witch at all in Verity's mind. To start with, she was far too young; then, she was stout of figure; lastly, she had black hair and no fingernails to speak of. However, looks can be deceptive.

"Come in! Come in!" cried the Green Witch, who was dressed in bright pink and had not a scrap of green about her person. Only the name of her house gave a clue as to her title.

"I think my friend needs your help more urgently than me," Verity told her, "I have pulled a bad tooth out of his mouth but it is infected and I wondered if some hypericum would help him?"

"Er...yes, and I think I have some tincture somewhere," replied the witch, looking very vague, "Would you like to

come in and your friend can go in the garden for now. The runner beans have too many leaves on them anyway and he may like the vines...well they rarely produce any grapes if he does trample them down. Only me here to chastise him."
"No black cat?" ventured Verity, half in jest.
"Made me sneeze," replied the witch, "so I sent him to my brother."

Verity was shocked but decided, since she needed help, to let that flow over her. The thought of letting Jet go was as painful as the loss of Frederick. Once inside the house, however, she put all thoughts of cats aside as she decided, instantly, there would not be room for even one paw.

Piles of papers, some yellow with age, seemed to be on every surface and the cupboards overflowed so that not a door would shut. Various weird and colourful toadstools littered the kitchen, at least Verity assumed it was the kitchen, and the floor was a death trap with boxes and items of clothing waiting to trip up the unwary.
"Yes, you start there," ordered the witch, "Avoid the red toadstools though as they give you fits...or is it kidney failure, I am not sure but don't touch them anyway..."

Verity had no intention of touching anything she did not have to as the dust of ages seemed to have settled thickly over all and she was not surprised the witch sneezed. Any poor cat residing at the house would never see the light of day.

She gingerly attempted to remove some mildewed magazines and was cheered by the witch's shout of joy.
"Ah, here it is Hypericum tincture! Will you take it to your friend or shall I?"
"I will, if you don't mind," replied Verity, anxious to get out of this jungle of junk and to see Garth before opening her sack of prizes for the witch, "Is there somewhere safe where he can go to heal? I came across him in the forest and if he returns there I fear he will be shot!"
"Heaven forbid!" cried the witch, "Well, I have a field behind here and I am on relatively good terms with the farmer as I saved his chickens from white spot....or was that

his fish? I can't remember but never mind. Let's get a lantern and go and put your friend in there. Then I presume you wish me to perform a spell for you?"
"Yes, I was not sure what I was collecting the prizes for but I see now they are part of the magic. I need to impress the dragon and barter with him for my true love's heart which is, at present, in a box waiting for the vampires to claim it."
"I can turn those prizes into jewels set to captivate the dragon completely, for he has an eye for anything colourful and sparkling! A mere puff of my wand and they are rubies! A tap of my finger and diamonds cascade forth! It really is that easy and quick!"

Having seen the total chaos in the so-called kitchen, Verity very much doubted that.

When Verity went out to see Garth, she could see the magic was fading from him and he would soon be a wild boar again. She stroked his head and he nuzzled her affectionately.
"You must never return to the forest, dear friend," she told him, "It seems the Green Witch is happy to look after you here and feed you all you desire. Please be good for her and do not gore any more humans who come your way."
"I shall not!" replied Garth, "You have shown me the way of compassion and peace and I shall tread that path now. However, my time to talk is short. Have you brought me anything for the abscess and the pain?"

Verity administered it to him and told him that tomorrow she would, hopefully, be on her way to the dragon with the jewels to attract his critical eye and that the Green Witch, whose name was Sally, would bring him his medicine after that.
"So it may be goodbye," she told the boar, as he swallowed the draught of hypericum and as he turned to her she saw he had become his former self and the wild look was back in his eye.
"You have all that you need here," she said, "Water, food and shelter and the witch, though slatternly and disorganised,

will make sure you get fed and cared for, I am sure." She sighed. The witch certainly cast no fear into Verity's heart but she gave no confidence either.

It was eight hours later and dawn had just crept across the autumn sky with a mixture of gold, pink and orange. When Verity had returned from helping Garth, she found the witch in a deep sleep, snoring loudly, and no amount of shaking her could induce a wakeful state. Thus Verity lay down on a very wonky settle, which she had to clear from mounds of clothes, papers and various articles that bore no resemblance to anything Verity recognised and, to her surprise, sleep came rapidly.

She awoke as the witch's huge clock chimed seven and, to her relief, the lady herself was stirring and trying to find misplaced objects for her morning toilet.

"Now, I had some soap somewhere near here yesterday morning and a towel. Were you sleeping on a towel by any chance, Verity?"

Verity got up and looked at the pile of rags she had put on the floor but not one of them could be described as a towel.

"No," she said, "At least I don't think so," She began to shake out the heap of material and Sally pounced on one blue piece, slightly bigger but just as crumpled as the rest.

"Ah! Here it is!" she cried, in triumph. She whisked it away and went out to get some water from her well.

An hour later, Sally was searching for some plates for breakfast and Verity was becoming impatient.

"I am not hungry," she told the witch.

"I made some bread yesterday," Sally told her, "and we are going to eat it. To say I made it is not actually true but I certainly got all the ingredients together and waved my wand. Usually when I do that it is inedible but when I tasted it for lunch yesterday, before you came, I managed to chew it so that is something."

Verity sighed and realised she must just put up with these constant delays. She was eager to show the witch all the prizes she had won and for Sally to start the spell, seeing as that was how she was going to bring forth the jewels. How long did a spell take? Verity had to be completely honest that she had never seen one being cast and had no clue. However, at the rate Sally worked it would be Christmas before the first word was uttered.

Finally, after the two women had eaten the driest bread Verity had ever tasted, Sally checked her guest's five prizes and, pronouncing them all correct, she began to search for the spell she needed.
"Can I assist you?" asked Verity, anxious that the spell was cast today but feeling that time was getting away from her. Frederick waited in the dark, shadowy corner of her mind.
"Oh it will be somewhere," replied the witch, "The last spell to summon the jewels was such a long time ago I do not know where I put the piece of paper. Now, let me think..."
Verity went into the garden and watched Garth, now back to being a wild animal, enjoying some apples and snuffling out slugs and snails in the field. She was not known for her patience but she realised the day was speeding away from her and that it would be tomorrow, at least, before she set off for the dragon. Going with the Green Witch as her ambassador did not fill her with confidence.
The afternoon came and went and still the witch searched but by then she had gone to her spare bedroom and various pieces of paper fluttered out of the window as she could be heard muttering,
"Now, that makes paper, why would I want any more of that? That brings a man into your life...well they are nothing but trouble!"
Verity picked up some of the pieces and tried to shuffle them tidily together but they kept coming and she gave up after a while and sat on the bench in the garden. No food or water was forthcoming once the witch was searching so Verity went to the well and, finding a beaker there, she thankfully drank deep of the pleasant-tasting water. She had just put the cup back when she heard Sally calling out and

she realised the witch had found what she had been looking for the past six hours. Now, finally, the spell could begin.

"I expected you to have a great cauldron into which you put everything," Verity told her, whilst the witch spent a fruitless hour searching for her wand.
"Is it magic?" Verity asked at length when it appeared Sally had given up.
"Oh no," replied the witch, "However, I rather liked its colour. Pink, you see, and the universal colour of love."

She began to thumb through another giant book, muttering to herself, and Verity despaired anything would ever come of this session.
"Do these spells take long?" she asked, when a lengthy silence had fallen. The witch shook her head.
"The ones I do daily take but a few minutes but what you require I have only done once or twice in my lifetime."
"You must have done it for my friend Adam Curlious," Verity told her, "He was a monk and needed his father's heart released."
"Very likely," Sally replied, "I make it a point to never remember names."

Verity was puzzled. She watched the witch arranging all the prizes she had collected on a black sheet. How hard had she fought for every one!
"Is the cloth part of the magic ritual?" she asked.
"Oh no," the witch told her, "Black is my second favourite colour and I like to be relaxed when I cast my spells. I have been known to fall asleep at the wheel, so to speak."

Verity raised her eyebrows. This was nothing like she thought it would be!

Sally turned all the items and then began to chant whilst Verity fell silent and watched as the witch moved the prizes from one end of the cloth to the other.
"I ask for clarity, spirits of the air. This young woman needs you. She has brought forth the five prizes you desired and I present them to you, each one a rarity in our beautiful country. How many miles she has travelled to capture these

pearls of the Welsh valleys! I ask you to look down favourably on her. She needs diamonds, she needs rubies, she needs emeralds, to take to the dragon as he will not release her loved one's heart without these precious jewels. Cascade them down on me and take these prizes, won by blood and sweat!" Her hands were uplifted to the heavens and her voice was getting louder and louder. Verity could hear her heart beating with fear. If the spirits did not answer her, how could she ever be Frederick's wife?

The witch appeared to go into a trance. Her eyes rolled from side to side and she began to speak with another voice. "Who desires these stones?" she cried, in deep tones, "Step forward so we may see you clearer! How great is your love for this man? What would you do for him?"

Verity walked forward, fear in her soul, but her anxiety to help her beloved was paramount.
"I came on this mission," she addressed the spirits, "without a thought for my safety, my only desire being to free the man I love from the affliction that ails him..."
"And would you walk through fire?"
"Yes, and the darkest part of hell too."
"Would you forsake all others for him?"
"I would. His life is mine and mine his, for we are joined in our souls and not even earthly death can separate us. He joined us by the ring he gave me and I wear it still on my finger but it encircles my heart."

There was a long silence but the witch threw her head around and Verity feared all was not going smoothly. However she saw Sally nod and produce a smile.
"You have answered well, young lady, and now we must look into that heart. We see fear there and doubts..."
"The doubts are my own personal weakness. I fear I am not good enough and I fear the dragon most of all."
"Why so? He is, after all, only a dragon and made of flesh and bones."
"But he is immortal and with one huff of his fiery breath he could burn me!"

"Have faith in the jewels we shall give you to carry to him. The dragon craves bright objects...they dazzle his eyes and provide light in the darkness. He is as frightened of the darkness as you are of him."

"So you will give me the jewels?" Verity almost shouted in relief, "My heart overflows with gratitude to you!"

Her eyes returned to the cloth and she could see the outline of her prizes beginning to fade. The witch was throwing her hands up in a gesture more of despair than of victory but slowly, definitely, Verity could see bright, sparkling objects forming against the black colour and as she looked, the jewels she craved came tumbling down – red, white and green. She gave a shout of joy and, as she did, the witch recovered her senses and, shaking her head, returned to her body from the astral plane where the benevolent spirits live.

Verity looked at her in amazement.

"You have done it!" she screamed, putting out her hands to encompass the shining stones, her eyes almost as bright as the jewels.

The Green Witch shrugged her shoulders.

"It all came back to me once I started," she admitted, "but fetch some water for a cup of tea, Verity, as all this astral travelling makes a body dry!"

CHAPTER FIFTEEN

It was the next day and, rested and jubilant, Verity set off to see the dragon with the Green Witch. So as to make a good impression, Sally was dressed head to toe in verdant green.
"I have never liked this colour," she told her guest as they began the long walk, "They say green is unlucky and when I first immersed myself in this hue I noticed my spells did not go to plan but when I changed and wore pinks, and even black, things went much more smoothly!"

Verity pondered on this as they walked and had to be honest that her faith in the Green Witch had been only slightly raised. She carried the precious jewels wrapped in deep orange muslin, dyed from the flowers in Sally's garden, and every so often she jiggled the bag just to hear them rattle.

Sally prattled on.
"The dragon is one for appearances," she told Verity, "He takes most things at face value but can be shallow in his judgement and he has the most awful temper when roused."

Verity shivered.
"He is the keeper of my beloved's heart," she murmured, "Therefore, we must not cross him but I fear this meeting more than any other as my happiness for the future depends on it. Can he refuse to give up the box I desire?"
"He can," replied the witch truthfully, "It may, indeed, take a bit of negotiation to free it, so we must only show him the diamonds first and keep his favourites, the red rubies, till last."

Verity sighed. Why was every step of the way so difficult? Yet Adam had borne this with a brave heart and so must she. "Do you have to go and see the dragon very often?" she asked now.

The Green Witch shrugged her shoulders.
"Not really," she replied, "It is a day's journey there and back and often a wasted one when he is in a bad mood. He

may not give us an audience and I have previously waited three days, only for him to shake his scaly head and turn me away!"

"Oh I hope that does not happen!" cried Verity, becoming even more worried, "My beloved could feel the stake at any moment and I promised to be back to the monastery before the winter spreads her white cloak over the land."

They journeyed on and their feet ate up the miles, although Verity was surprised that the witch did not cast a spell to get them there more quickly.

"The dragon would not like that," Sally told her, "Everyone must arrive on their own two feet. No winged horses or magic carpets would be admitted to the Palace of Reflections. The guards are very strict on that."

"Who are these guards?" asked Verity, "Will they admit us?"

"By and large they are goblins and elves the dragon has pressed into working for him after he destroyed their woodlands. He is clumsy to a fault."

Verity disliked him more and more.

"He must be in league with the vampires to hold the hearts they possess," she told the witch, angrily.

"The dragon would do anything for jewels and he fills his palace with them so that the dark is warded off no matter what time of year it is. He dreads the winter, and autumn, too, brings sadness to his heart, so do not expect to find him sanguine or even pleasant. The vampires would have him as their gatekeeper and they shower jewels and precious stones on him for guarding the boxes. We have to catch his eyes with brightness and colour and I hope our diamonds will do that but if not, we can back it up with the rubies. The emeralds he holds as trash but mixed in with the red they should please his temper and lift his spirits. After all, what is a million pounds of shine for just one small box?"

Verity hoped and prayed Sally spoke the truth.

Up and up they climbed and Verity's head spun with the height and fatigue too. Reaching the summit they rested on a

green lawn and the witch wondered what to conjure up for lunch.
"Bread? Or a nice leg of lamb?" she queried, raising her pink wand which she had found, just before they left, among a pile of mouldy magazines.
"A nice leg of lamb should be left on the animal," Verity told her, shuddering, "Bread for me, or nuts or fruit please. I do not partake of the flesh of others, animals or people, as they are all equal. A life is a life to me and deserves respect."

The witch acknowledged her views and began to wave her wand around and chant. For a while nothing appeared to happen and then a packet of something fell out of the air and, splitting, cascaded its contents all over them.
"Soap flakes!" said Sally in disgust, "Now, how did I get that wrong?"

Shaking her encrusted hair free of them, Verity hoped that it was not a bad omen for the visit.

Two hours later, they had arrived and Verity craned her neck to see the huge stone castle hung about with jewels of every shape and colour. Mirrors backed some of the larger pieces so their refulgence was doubled and, in the bright light of an autumn sun, they appeared like a beacon on a hillside that burnt with great power.

The moat was filled not with water but with even more jewels and Verity doubted their offering would be accepted. Surely the dragon had enough! The drawbridge was down and they began walking over it when a few small goblins scuttled up to them and demanded to know what they were doing here.

The most important and largest had a piece of paper and a quill pen and his minions carried bottles of ink which he dipped the nib into then wrote in a flourishing hand.
"Strangers," he murmured, as he formed the words, "Two women. Both young and one dressed in green...Er...do you have an appointment please?"

The Green Witch shook her head.

"We do not need one," she told the goblin, who was dressed in the most flamboyant orange that dazzled their eyes. "Everybody needs one," he retorted and his minions tutted, "The dragon will not see anyone without an appointment."
"He will see me," declared Sally, "I am the Green Witch and you are to go tell him I have some jewels for him in exchange for a favour, and they make this lot on display look like coloured glass!"
"I am sorry but you are not on the list for today," said the goblin, "Green Witch? No. Nor a purple one or a red one...no visitors the dragon said and besides, he is sleeping after his luncheon and cannot be disturbed until three."
"Then we will wait until he wakes up," replied the Green Witch, "We are in no hurry but we will NOT be leaving here without an audience, I can tell you. This lady has come all the way from England to see him!"

The goblins tittered.

"I don't care if she has come all the way from the moon, she still can't see the dragon without an appointment!" came the reply back.

Sally was losing patience. She seized the paper and the pen and wrote in her large, firm hand,
'Miss Verity Whittle and the Green Witch 3pm.'

Handing the paper back to the larger goblin she said in a loud, powerful voice,
"There! You have forgotten to add us to your list today and as such, if I tell the dragon, he will throw you out and relegate you to damp tree trunks and the Wood of the Lost."

The goblins looked at each other and tutted, clearly unsure of how to proceed.

"We have an appointment now," Sally told them, "Please make sure you call us at three and we would like to come in and rest until then. Some of your acorn tea would not go amiss. Well, what are you waiting for? Do you want me to tell the dragon how you treated us after we got an appointment? He will not be pleased!"

The goblins looked at the paper.

"Well it does say your names now and there is no one else for three o'clock," acknowledged the bigger one. He turned the paper for the other three to see.

"Are you sure you did not write this yourself?" asked one.

Verity smiled as she saw the witch cross her fingers behind her back and deny it.

"I merely folded the paper to this afternoon's appointments and, as you can see, there we are..."

The goblins looked incredulous but could not doubt the names on the list. They ran away over the drawbridge and the two women followed, Sally dusting off her hands in hauteur.

"Goblins!" Verity heard her utter under her breath, "The lowest of the low and as much brain activity as you would find in a slug! Easily fooled and of course, to the dragon, cheap labour!"

Verity looked up at the high Welsh castle as they entered it and her heart beat fast with both excitement and dread. Somehow, through subterfuge, they had their audience with the dragon!

A number of clocks struck the hour of three in the Palace of Reflections and the Green Witch stood up and stretched. Mirrors to her left and right showed her raiment was neat and tidy and she put a comb through her hair and advised Verity to do the same.

"Then we face the dragon with confidence, safe in the knowledge that we appear tidy and smart, for he hates anything slovenly and may reject us purely for our attire!" she said.

Verity felt decidedly scruffy. Months of travelling with the same few gowns had done nothing for the colour or material of the dresses and she feared there were holes in the seams and hems. She voiced her fears to Sally and showed her the threadbare material.

Sally frowned.

"Keep behind me then," she advised, "and let me do most of the talking. Tuck the ragged part of your dress under your shoes and all will be well!"

"But they have holes in them as well!" Verity wailed.

Sally shrugged.

"It cannot be helped," she said with a sigh, "He must take you as you are, as I presume your other dresses are worse?"

Verity undid her bag and pulled a couple out but they were caked with mud after her last dalliance through the forest, so she tried to make the one she was wearing look as decent as she could. Sally brushed the front and back and the small tears in the fabric were only visible when up close.

The goblins had been hospitable and they had dined on toadstool bread and quince jelly washed down with a weird sort of herb tea that Verity thought tasted of soap but was obliged to drink for politeness. Now she felt vaguely sick but today she would finally know if Frederick's heart was going to be returned to her or not. All the work of the past weeks and months were either going to pay off or be fruitless. She saw herself returning to the monastery with her head low and her hopes totally dashed but she tried to obliterate such pictures and replace them with the jubilation of victory.

"And you are certain that, if we do obtain my beloved's heart, you know the spell to restore it to his body and drive the vampire curse out?" she asked once more.

Sally very patiently nodded and replied she had her book of charms with her and knew exactly what to do. Remembering the cascading soap flakes, Verity did not feel easy about this but she had no time to say anything more as the tallest goblin was calling them forward. They left their small room and journeyed up a long, narrow corridor festooned with mirrors, every one encrusted with jewels and coloured stones. The refulgence from the brightly clustered objects was amazing and Verity whispered that it would be everlasting daylight here, with no vestige of darkness entering the palace.

"That is the dragon's weakness," Sally whispered back, "He is terrified of the advent of night and whoever heard of a dragon scared of the dark?"

Verity was somewhat reassured by this. It gave him a human side, no longer the great, immortal, scaled beast but someone with a heart and, in that heart, imperfections.

They journeyed on, always flanked by the goblins as though they were prisoners in a sea of light. Eventually they came to a huge room with high ceilings and, craning her neck, Verity could see that every inch of space was taken up by jewels of various colours and sizes. Blue, aquamarine, red, pink, yellow, green...the list went on... and always the backdrop of gold to enhance them all.

"The dragon's chamber is off this room," the Green Witch told her, "So he may appear at any moment but be prepared for his temper, which is known to be fierce." They heard a sudden sound, like the roar of a distant typhoon, and the goblins scattered and ran off as though the sight of their master was too much for them to bear. The ground shook beneath them but Verity was intrigued rather than frightened. Her first glimpse of a dragon! Would he be like the winged serpent of her storybooks or would he portray a softer and more human persona?

"Who disturbs the red dragon and wakes him from his slumbers, I ask you?" boomed a voice and Verity saw the room fill up with scarlet scales and claws, all shaking as though with anger.

"I am the last great dragon of Wales and I deserve and command respect!"

The Green Witch motioned Verity to curtsey, which she did although her eyes were on the dragon the whole time and his black, beady eye intrigued her.

"Honoured sir," began the Green Witch but Verity, overcome with emotion as to this fabled beast, butted in.

"Dear Dragon," she said, "I have travelled so many miles and all for this moment. I have collected five prizes with great hardship and been out of my motherland for months, it seems. Now I stand before you, humble and grateful for this audience, as you hold, in the palm of your...er...foot, the ability to make me happy or miserable for the rest of my life!"

The dragon moved a little closer and asked her her name. "Verity Whittle, sir. My beloved is under the spell of the vampires and cannot marry me until you give me his heart in a wooden box to take back to the monastery where he resides."

The dragon raised his enormous head and shook his scaled body as though ridding it of sleep.

"What is this to me?" he roared, "Am I not the keeper of thousands of hearts for the vampires? What do I care that they drink human blood and bite the unwary. They have to live."

"But they are Undead, sir, and, as such, they leave our loved ones in limbo, neither with us nor in heaven and no grave to visit and mourn over. My Frederick is sentenced to eternity craving and lusting after blood."

The dragon extended a foot and rapped his claws on the jewelled skirting board.

"This is what I get for being the gatekeeper," he told Verity, "Can you match such an offer? This is the Palace of Reflections and my aim is to fill it with every precious stone known to man!" He swished his tail perilously close to Verity but she never moved.

"I know, sir, you are frightened of the dark but it is purely the absence of light and, come the morning, dawn will break anew!"

The dragon was furious and the Green Witch tried to make amends.

"Forgive my friend," she cried, "She has never met a dragon before and does not know how to behave!"

The dragon gave a snort and some fire curled around his nostrils.

"Are you aware, Miss Whittle, that I could destroy you with just one blow of my breath and you would be a blackened offering, fit only to be buried to enrich the earth?"

"Yes, sir, and I tell you, if I can never have the man I love, I would gladly let you breathe upon me rather than face the long years ahead without him by my side!"

The dragon was confused. Usually, mere mortals grovelled at his feet and cried for mercy when he threatened them with fire.

"Have you so little regard then for your life?" he asked her.
"I exist without Frederick in my life, sir, I do not live. He is a good, nay, a great man and he has the power to make me so happy! Please, I beg you, give me back his heart. I was terrified when I knew my only chance of happiness was to come here and face a dragon but, now I am here, my love for Frederick eclipses every other emotion! You live in the light, sir, but imagine you dwelt in the dark as I do, and am doomed to do forever unless you help me! You can bring the light into my life by giving me my beloved's heart."

The Green Witch could see the dragon was utterly bemused and she came forward now and told him that they had gifts to trade for the box.

"We have jewels so fine, sir, they will make these around you look like coloured glass!" she told the creature.

The dragon softened a bit.

"Let me see them," he said, with a shake of his tail that sounded like a rumble of distant thunder, "I have found a ceiling in an anteroom where the jewels are not as thick as I would like and they may do to fill a gap."

Verity opened her bag and showed him the diamonds first, which shone with all their power, and quite outdid the stones around them.

"Not enough," said the dragon, "I need more."

Verity showed him the emeralds but he sneered, showing long, sharp teeth.

"The harbingers of doom I say, although I do love their colour…have you more?"

The Green Witch nodded to her companion and Verity unwrapped the rubies, which dazzled them with their red light.

The dragon was elated.

"The very stones I have been searching for to illuminate the anteroom ceiling!" he cried. Slowly, he reached out a scaly foot and sent a claw round the largest.

"Ah...feel its warmth," he crooned, "You talk about life, Miss Whittle, but I tell you, it is here..."

"Yes, sir, for you, but I would swap all these precious stones for just one moment with my beloved! To me, they are worthless glass compared to his heart! However, they are yours if you can give us his box and break the spell!"

The dragon thought long and hard.

"The diamonds are fine, the emeralds I can live without but the rubies...I cannot pass them by!" and he brought his foot up to his beady eye and gazed into the beauty of the ruby he held.

Verity felt he was weakening.

"Sir, how you regard the ruby is how I regard Frederick! Can you understand me? To you, the beauty of the universe is held in the bright red stone but for me, it is dark and cold! We make our own light, sir, by our actions and we create our own darkness and fear too! Frederick IS my ruby, my diamond, my emerald! With Frederick by my side, I will never be afraid of the dark!"

The dragon continued to gaze at the ruby as though his whole life depended on it.

"With these beauties by my side, no trace of darkness will enter the Palace of Reflections!" he said. Verity felt an affinity with the huge, scaled creature before her. How fearful he was of the light leaving his life and how fearful she was of facing the darkness that Frederick's absence immersed her in! He might be a mythological being but he stood before her as mortal as herself.

Unable to stop herself, she leant forward and stroked the dragon on the nose. He leapt back in horror and sent a small table spinning into the air.

"Who dares to touch the last great dragon of Wales!" he roared, shaking his head in some confusion.

Verity was not to be put down.

"Sir, I stroked you. It was a friendly gesture from one being to another to show I understand your fear, because it is my fear too! Together we can help each other! You need the rubies to enlighten your life and keep the darkness away and I need Frederick's heart to lift the darkness in my life! I bestow these gifts on you, will you not bestow the gift of light on me, too?"

The dragon was totally confused. Besides which, he had rather enjoyed the stroke and he said now, in a curious voice, "What did you do to me?"

In answer, Verity stepped up to his huge head and repeated the stroke a few times on both his nose and the back of his head. His eyes lit up and he turned to regard her.

"Miss Whittle, you have won me over! Just one more thing I ask of you. Can the goblins be taught, brainless wonders that they are, to do this stroking thing to me?"

Down and down they went into the vaults underneath the castle and the darkness was suffocating and real. The leading goblin had a lamp but to Verity, at the back of the queue of fairy folk, it was barely distinguishable, just a blob of brightness up ahead.

Despite the victory she had scored, she felt nervous. What if Frederick's heart could not be found? What if it had never been here?

Have I not seen it in my dreams, she soothed herself, in a rosewood box covered by thorns and briars?

They reached a locked door and the tallest goblin took forth a bunch of keys and, after a few wrong tries, succeeded in opening it. A foul stench of misery hit Verity. Years and years of misery, eternities for those hearts possessed by the vampires and with not a soul to set out to reclaim them! The sadness of the situation washed over her and she shed a tear.

"You will be sure to give me the correct one, won't you?" she asked the goblin, who bade her stand back whilst he searched. The other three watched her every move as though they expected her to bolt off with God knows what. She felt distinctly uncomfortable.

"Frederick, Frederick, Frederick," quoted the searching goblin.

"Pyne," shouted Verity, fearing she would get someone else's heart and be doomed to repeat the experience all over again. Heaven forbid, she told herself.

"Frederick Pyne, ah...a relatively new one and the dust not even accumulated on his box," said the goblin, retreating from the room with a dark brown box.

Verity put out her hands for it but the goblin snatched it back and said it had to be shown to the dragon first.

"He will want to inspect it," he told Verity, "He loses jewels once it has gone and thus, we lose wages too. It is not a happy time for us."

"I have done the penance and paid the price for it," Verity told him firmly, "I will not lose it now, come what may."

The goblin ran ahead in the darkness and the others followed, Verity struggling to keep up. Once they reached the light again, she was shown back to the Green Witch who sat in a giant antechamber admiring the view of hill and dale.

"Apparently the dragon needs to inspect it," she told Sally.

The Green Witch nodded her head.

"It is seemly," she replied, "The dragon needs to do that as he keeps an army of idiots on a meagre wage and what do they care if they give you the wrong box?"

However, after only a few minutes the tall goblin came back bearing the box and told them the dragon had released it and now they needed to leave the Palace of Reflections.

"We shall be glad to do so," Verity told him, taking the box and pressing it to her heart. A part of Frederick that was not possessed by the vampires! How precious it was!

Down the steps of the great building they went and across the drawbridge. The jewels were shining brightly in the evening sun and Verity paused on a small hillock to look back.

"When this is all over, will I think I dreamt it?" she murmured to herself, "Will I think I journeyed to Wales and found Frederick whole and well?"

The Green Witch understood her and left her to stand for a minute, face to the wind, ruminating on all she had achieved in the past months. Then they moved on and the palace disappeared in the growing dusk of evening. Verity turned around but it could not be seen any more. It was as it should be and she left it in the shades of darkness, knowing that the light would glow eternal in that strange place, where hardly an inch was not covered by jewels.

CHAPTER SIXTEEN

"We must make our way to the monastery as quickly as we can," Sally told Verity, as darkness stalked them and the trees became waving arms, casting their leaves aside in the evening winds, "The vampires will know we have Frederick's heart and they will try to reclaim it!"

Verity had not been aware of that and she remarked now that she had hoped to retrace her steps and visit Rose once more, if only for an hour.

"There is no chance of that," Sally told her, "Night draws on and the creatures who flourish in its shadows come forth. They will smell the blood in the box and they will desire to feed. We are in danger every step of the way until daylight comes. I will try to magic us to the monastery and call up the winged horse but the vampires may block my spell."

"Can they do that once we attain the monastery steps?" Verity asked anxiously.

"No, we have sanctuary there but it is a long journey and may take us a day if we have to walk," the Green Witch replied.

They began to stride briskly through the darkness but every creak of a tree or flurry of fallen leaves alarmed them. Sally drew forth her book of spells and tried to conjure up help but her efforts fell flat. After about an hour, Verity worried they were being followed but, apart from a fleeting shadow, every time she turned around nothing was visible. They reached the outskirts of a large forest and paused to drink from a stream.

Luckily the moon was full, the harvest moon as Sally put it, and to banish the intermittent darkness she managed to magic up a lantern which diminished their fear a little. Verity's thoughts were with Andrew; would he come to her if the vampires struck or should she rub the staff and bring forth the tiger? Surely Sally's spells would be a match for the bloodsuckers?

They braved the forest and crept from tree to tree but the sight of one or two bats filled them with foreboding. Verity clutched Frederick's heart to her chest and vowed that, no matter what, she would not part with it. She was so near to getting her beloved back…

Suddenly Sally stopped, hearing voices in the next clearing.

"Shh…," she warned Verity, "we must hide here by this tree until we know who walks the oncoming path."

They ducked down, barely daring to breathe, and the silence was audible. Verity was just going to say she did not hear anything when two dark figures came past them and both women froze. It was obvious from their talk that they were out hunting the bloodsuckers but that told the travellers that vampires definitely lived in this vicinity, so their relief was short lived.

"And one of them had seven cows from William's farm last night. Well, I say one of them, more likely quite a few judging by the blood that was drained from the animals."

"Only one has actually been seen," came the reply, "However where there is one, there will be others and at every bite they create more. Thankfully no humans have been taken so far but unless we stake these evil predators, I fear people from the village will be affected and then how will we cope?"

The men passed them by and Verity breathed a sigh of relief. Sally was trying, with all her might, to summon up a mode of transport.

"In the darkness of the night
Bring us now a source of light,
Pegasus, we need your wings
Are you where the daylight brings
Dawn's sweet freedom to the skies?
Come to save us, our hope dies.
White winged horse answer my call
Fly us home, save one and all!"

This verse she repeated three times and after the third time, Verity heard a strange rushing in the air. Fearing it was a vampire she covered her face but Sally stood tall and erect and let out a delighted cry.
"Well, I may have got the actual mode of transport wrong but we can certainly travel in style now!" she told Verity, who opened her eyes to view a flying carpet waiting for them above the treetops. Both women hurried into the next clearing and the giant carpet descended so that they could climb onto it.

Up, up, up they flew and the earth was a minuscule dot below them, the chilled air thrust icy fingers at their faces and Verity was glad of her cloak but poor Sally only had her green attire and she shivered.
"To the monastery," she whispered to the wind and the carpet flew faster and faster over the green and gentle valleys of Wales. The final leg of their journey was reached and the end was surely in sight.

"I cannot believe we are on our way home," Verity told the Green Witch as the carpet sped towards its destination. "It seems years since I left Frederick and embarked on this mission of mercy. My heart tells me he is still alive but how Lawrence has coped with him, I do not know. I am sure Adam has helped out but the poor man must be exhausted. He was angry with me for attempting this journey so I pray he will be glad to see us."
"We are not back yet," replied Sally and, as she said this, she felt the carpet take a nosedive and begin its descent to the ground. Her face was troubled.
"But we must be near for the carpet to fly lower, surely?" Verity said hopefully.

Sally had misgivings about this but kept silent. She tried a spell to force the carpet to gain height but it did not seem to be working. The carpet merely shuddered and dropped like a stone so that the two women had to hold on very tight.

Once the ground was in sight, dimly through the darkness, the carpet began to flip over and Verity and Sally plummeted to the earth, falling - luckily - onto soft ground. Verity's bag fell on her head but she began to scrabble about to find her staff, lost in the dim light.

After a few minutes searching she had not found it and she worried it had been flung far and wide. The carpet had vanished and they were in the midst of a wood which Sally said they must get out of, as she feared the vampires could be about.

"Someone overruled my spell and brought us down here," she told Verity, "My magic seems useless now and the winged horse has closed his ears to us. We must make our way on foot and be vigilant. It wants a few hours till sunrise and the bloodsuckers could be active. Luckily the moon is still up and we can follow her but we must keep to the shadows."

"But I cannot leave without finding my staff!" wailed Verity, casting her eyes here and there, "Old Mr Curlious gave it to me and I must return it once we get to the monastery. Please help me look!"

Sally gave in and they searched again but nothing was visible. Time and time again Sally tried her magic to locate the staff but every time her spells were useless. She feared the vampires were near and she told Verity that, staff or not, they had to move on.

"But that stick has been my protection for the whole journey!" Verity cried, "How can I lose it now?"

"Ssh..." warned Sally, "The trees have ears. We must get out of here and quickly. I do not know which way to go but I know we are in danger if we stay."

They left the site and went northward, which Sally felt was the right direction at least. They saw foxes, badgers and numerous owls with mournful cries but nothing more sinister. Verity left the box in her bag which she carried on her back but fear was all around them and the night was dark.

Eventually they left the wood behind and the eerie trees thinned out and were replaced by open grassland where at least they could see any foe approaching them. Verity's heart beat so loudly that she thought the whole world would hear it and her chest was tight and painful. Sally tried her spells again but nothing happened and she sensed her powers were being drained. The moon was their only ally.

They breasted a hill and descended into a valley and Sally thought the monastery was very near but at a crossroads she did not know which road to take. Her head was buzzing as she tried to tune in and just when she had decided to take the most northerly track, Verity gave a scream. There, to the left of them, walked two figures, dressed all in black, the moon revealing their red eyes.

Sally stood in front of Verity as the figures approached and began to chant a spell for protection.

"Who tries to disturb our walk with the rhymes of witchcraft?" asked the nearest one, smiling and showing long fangs that were smeared with blood.

"You are lucky that we have feasted well tonight," said the second figure. "However, we know what you have stolen and we want it back!"

Despite her fear, Verity was determined not to give up her prize.

"We have stolen nothing," she shouted, "I have worked for my beloved's heart and it is no longer yours. It is mine."

The first vampire grabbed Sally and flung her to the ground, standing over her and showing his teeth in a demonic sneer.

"One bite and your friend joins us," he told Verity. He was close enough now for her to smell his fetid breath and the familiar stench brought back painful memories of Alphonso.

"You shall not have it," she maintained, "I have broken the spell and you do not have the right to claim it back!"

"The dragon is weak and easily distracted by gems and sunshine," replied the second vampire, "However you will not find us so pliable! I can find room in my stomach for a little more blood. Surrender the box or else face the future with us for all eternity!"

His teeth were perilously near Sally's neck and her face was terrified. The moon came out and Verity gazed upon its beauty, praying for some intervention. Where was the staff now when she needed its ferocious tiger? And then there was...

"Andrew! Andrew! If you are there, as my angel, please, please come and help me!" she cried, raising her arms to the skies, "I really need you now!"

The two vampires smiled and mentioned that angels were a figment of the imagination but that they were real.

"Feel us, touch us," they sneered as they seized hold of Verity and she screamed loudly and prepared for their evil bite...

Then suddenly, out of nowhere, she heard the flap of wings, distant but coming closer. Both the vampires looked up as though they expected more of their kind to join them but a different sort of aviator filled the dark skies.

"Andrew!" screamed Verity, as the archangel descended and stood between the two women.

"St Michael!" shouted Sally, recognising the figure instantly. The long blue and silver cloak was round his shoulders and his eyes smouldered. Instinctively, the two vampires backed off. The goodness and purity of his presence revolted them.

The archangel threw angel dust in their faces and they screamed aloud and took to the skies, vanishing as quickly as they had come so that both women breathed a sigh of relief.

"Oh Andrew," murmured Verity, running up to him and touching his healing cloak, "I have lost my precious staff. It fell, we know not where, when the vampires broke Sally's spell and the carpet plunged downwards. I don't suppose you could use your all-seeing eyes and find it for me?"

"Hmm...what about me, Verity? Now the vampires' power has waned, my magic should be able to seek it out!" Sally told her, feeling rather left out.

Andrew smiled and produced the very article from his robe, handing it to Verity with a smile.

"Save your magical powers, Green Witch, for they will be needed to secure Frederick's heart into his body. I was flying over and saw the staff in the crook of a tree, a few feet above the ground. I recognised it at once. The night's power diminishes, ladies, and you must be on your way. My cloak surrounds you and the way is clear. Take the next left at the fork and in four miles you will reach the road to the monastery. I will be watching over you and no-one will hurt you now."

Suddenly, in a whirr of wings and blue with silver, he was gone and only the perceptive murmur of the air remained behind him. Verity kissed the staff in joy and the two women took the road Andrew had pointed out. In a couple of hours, maybe less, they would be back from the most perilous journey Verity had ever taken in her life and the monastery would be opening its doors to welcome them.

"I am sure the first light of dawn is in the sky," Sally said hopefully, as they followed Andrew's instructions and saw the monastery in the distance. Verity increased her pace and her heart beat fast at the thought of her beloved, restored, standing before her.
"And you are sure, that is, you are confident, you can perform the ritual to make me the happiest of women?" she said to the Green Witch as they breasted the last hill between them and home.
"I have to admit, it is not something I do every day," Sally admitted,"but I have my book and my wand and you have the heart, so do not fear, Verity, all will be well."
"But what if you make some sort of mistake, as you have done in the past?" Verity wailed. Life was so very near her grasp but one error could banish it forever…
"Hmm….the soap flake incident was a very easy mistake to make. You see the spell for that is just one shake of the wand to the left away from another."
"Will you need to rest and sleep first then to ensure you are in peak condition?"
"Sadly that is not possible. The heart needs to be back in the body before midday or it could fail on that alone. We must start at once. I do see a vestige of sun I am sure!"
"And at that Frederick will calm and sleep. Must we drug him whilst you do it? Can I be there? Will you go in alone?"

Anxiety was making Verity gabble and her hands shook as the venerable building grew closer.

"I shall sedate him with valerian and some other herbs I carry in a pouch on my belt. You can be there, but I ask it is only you and perfect silence is preserved. Your thoughts must be positive ones of seeing him whole and well again."

"I shall have no others," promised Verity, "My heart will be filled with hope for the future."

The hill was steep but they could see their goal and before too long, they were walking up the path and back to the tree Verity had regarded as she left for her dangerous journey. "Brave sentinel – I have come home to you!" she told the tree, running to it and caressing its worn bark, "I am so glad to be back and with the prize I set out to attain all those months ago!"

She hurried forward to the familiar path and, reaching out her hand, she touched the cool, smooth monastery stone. "Sanctuary!" she cried. No one could take Frederick's heart away from her now. It was home.

CHAPTER SEVENTEEN

The door swung open before them and an air of calm and quiet pervaded the long, narrow hallway, backed by the melodic sound of voices singing in the dawn. Verity's eyes filled with tears as the familiar smell of damp and humanity washed over her.

She clutched Frederick's heart to her chest and whispered, "You are home now, we are home..."

The chanting got louder as a door opened and closed, then footsteps rang out on the corridor.

"Verity!"

It was Adam. She looked up and called out to him, "We are back, my friend, and we have the Green Witch to conduct the ceremony but we need to hurry! How is Frederick? I trust he is still alive?"

"If you mean, is he still Undead, then yes he is," replied Lawrence, appearing suddenly from the shadows, "He has taken at least ten years of my life away!"

Verity rushed to embrace them both, handing over the precious box to Sally but she felt Lawrence draw back, although Adam was as warm as ever.

"Come this way then," replied Lawrence, fair pushing her aside, "The sooner this tomfoolery is over, the better."

Verity followed the monk and Lawrence down the dark stairs but a shaft of sunlight made merry on the walls and she blessed its brightness.

"Your ouzel bird and the pigeon arrived safely to foretell of your delay, but the fact that you were alive as well," Adam told her.

"I hope you housed them kindly and they are still alive?" Verity asked.

"Oh yes, the pigeon has settled with our doves and the ouzel bird makes merry in the garden and eats the late fruits," the monk told her, but Lawrence sighed.

"Enough of your talk of birds," he cried, "You have been away far too long, Verity, and my patience has been sorely

tried! I was for staking Frederick upwards of a hundred times but Adam fought your corner and thwarted me at every turn!"
"I am here now, Lawrence, and so is Sally and this will be over in the next hour," Verity promised.
"Witches!" swore Lawrence, "It is a wonder you allow one over the threshold of this holy and sacred place, Adam. Are you not defiling God by doing so?"
"If there was another way, I would take it, believe me, but I know from experience there is not. Peace, my brother and give the Green Witch a chance!" from Adam.

They had reached the cellar and a rhythmic moaning coming from the cell told them Frederick was falling into a dream filled sleep. Sally affirmed this was good.
"And now I must ask everyone but Verity to leave me," she said.

Adam gave Verity a squeeze of the arm and wished her good luck but Lawrence handed over the keys silently and went on his way.

Verity let her eyes travel to where he climbed the stairs and sighed. Adam, following her train of thought, said, "He has been pushed to the edge of hell and back by Frederick's conduct! A vampire hunter, now one of the great Undead! It defies reason and it does not sit easy with the man. He is possessed by an opposing force, one that he hunted down and slew in life. He is a tormented soul and has behaved far worse than my father did..."
"I acknowledge the great and wonderful thing Lawrence has done in caring for his friend. He has shown loyalty beyond that which I could expect but I love Frederick and my heart cannot let him go."

A hushed silence fell and then Frederick cried out in his sleep. Verity was reduced to tears.

Adam left them and the Green Witch began to unpack her small bag that had been attached to her belt.
"Valerian for peace, Myrrh for cleansing and Frankincense to open the soul....Sage to purge," she chanted, as she produced the items one by one.

"We have to get Frederick to take these, Verity, and that is where you come in. He trusts you and as much as he wants you he knows the time is not right. He is more a man than a vampire until darkness taints the sky once more."

Sally made a concoction of the herbs and added some sparkling liquid. She poured the mixture into a goblet that was at hand and asked Verity to go in and present it to Frederick.

"Let him hear your voice but do not stay in there," Sally told her, "Speak to him and reassure him but do not delay as my magic might not be able to protect you if the change does come upon him. Remember how my spells faded against the might of the vampires..."

Verity was very scared but she took the vessel and the keys and approached her beloved. As she turned the lock he seemed to come to a little and remarked that he was dreaming as he saw his betrothed before his eyes.

"You do not dream, my darling," Verity said to him, although she shook with fear and kept her eyes on the door. "I truly am come home to you but I need you to do something before I can be yours."

Frederick's face lit up.

"You are come to be mine then! In these past months you refused my bite so often. Offer me your neck..."

"You must drink this first," she told him, receiving courage from his mild tone and lazy demeanour, "Then I will truly be yours!"

The vessel changed hands and, as it did, Frederick grabbed Verity's fingers and attempted to kiss them but she snatched her hand back and protested,

"You promised to take this first, Frederick, and unless you do I must leave you forever, trapped in the abyss of the twilight world..."

"I cannot take the sun!" he cried, gazing upwards as though it shone on him, "You must join me in the dark where the night creatures walk..."

"I will, I will," she assured him, "Drink. Drink and then we will be together!"

She was pleased to see he did as asked and she drew off whilst the draught took effect. He appeared not to notice her departure and Sally quickly took the box with the heart in and went through the door with her small spell book in hand and the pink wand.

"Courage, Verity, courage!" she whispered as she passed her friend, "I want you to sit and close your eyes and visualise Frederick whole and well and the curse of the vampire no more upon him. Can you do that?"

Verity's eyes were full of tears but she affirmed she could and, leaving the Green Witch to her spell, she sat on the floor and began to say to herself,

"Frederick, may you be whole and well again.
Frederick, may the curse leave you now..."

Her eyes tightly shut, she saw Frederick rising, as if from the grave, healed and calm, the wild look gone from his eyes and in her mind she saw him turn to her and say,

"I have been asleep a long time, my darling, and my dreams have been terrible. They have haunted me day and night and the smell of blood is in my nostrils but it goes and is replaced by the perfume of flowers. The curse is leaving me, the curse is leaving me..."

The Green Witch noticed that Frederick had slumped upon his bed and she knew she had to work fast in order to facilitate the change and put his heart back into his body. Would it reject it? Would the herbs cleanse and open the system ready to receive the life force? Her hands shook but she brought the heart forth and noticed, as she laid it on the man's chest, that it began to beat.

"It recognises him," she said aloud, "It knows it is nearly home!"

Opening her book, she began to recite a spell, waving her wand around Frederick's body and he twisted and turned as though in torment.

"Hell opens one more page for you
So vampire spirit pass on through,
The Devil makes his men of clay

Enter these men and pave the way…
The heart that's here pumps with pure love,
I symbolise it as a dove…."

Frederick cried out and gnashed his teeth and the Green Witch took a step back.
"Send Frederick your love now!" she screamed to Verity, sensing the man was stirring and the vampire in him was now wide awake.

Verity rained down as much love on him as she could and Frederick began to writhe as though in agony.
"No, no, no!" he screamed.

Verity began to doubt but Sally urged her on.
"Carry on, Verity, do not stop, for it is vital we drive this demon out of him. His soul is open and we must act now!"
"Love, love, love," chanted Verity, lost in a bright pink light, "Love, love, love!"

Frederick foamed at the mouth and the blood ran from him but Verity kept on,
"Love, love, love!"

Sally began to spin around the writhing body and touched him on the chest and temples with the wand.
"Leave, leave," she chanted,
"The possessed spews out power and hate
And pink love wanders in,
She overcomes the fear and doubt
And cleanses you of sin."

"Fight it, Frederick, fight it. You want this love, you want Verity as your wife. May your orbs dance with pink. The bad blood leaves you. It leaves you!"

From Frederick's eyes, mouth and ears ran black blood and Sally knew she was nearly there. One final push whilst the herbs had him in their power.
"Love, Verity, love! Increase the power! This is your man and you must fight for him now! The vampires want him. Are you going to let them take him? His heart yearns to

cleave to his body once more, it moves, it vibrates on his chest! Help him!"

"Love, love, love," chanted Verity, doused in the pink light she was creating, "Let love take you, Frederick, love. Breathe out hate and doubt and breathe in love!"

A pink mist was forming over Frederick's face and the black blood was gone, run away into the ether to be dissolved and made pure again. For everything returns in one form or another and energy, even though it was created as bad, can be washed as pure white as milk.

Sally's face took on the form of the vampire and her teeth lengthened and her ears grew huge as she took the evil away. "I exude love, you cannot live in me!" she cried, "Get gone to the Lord of the Underworld! Get gone!"

"For Hades waits with molten streams
And fever rends the air,
The Lord of Darkness wants your soul
Eternity is there.
Not on this mortal plane, this earth,"

She flung her hands up as the vampire spirit left her with a rush of wings and the stench of evil

"Hell take your soul...love will give birth
To purity, a spirit, white
No more to wander 'witched at night,
No more to crave blood's cold, red mist.
By vampire curses you've been kissed
But love has ousted out the pain
Brave Frederick be yourself again!"

She screamed the last line out and collapsed on the floor. Verity rushed to the cell, unsure of what to do. Sally had given her all and now lay prostrate, her breathing deep and rasping, as she began to recover.

As Verity turned her attention to Frederick, she saw the heart was no longer on his chest. A mark, like a small cross, was visible through his torn shirt and she saw he began to rise and make his way towards her. The door was open and Verity was primed to run, when Frederick looked down at Sally on the floor and wrinkled up his nose.

"I never could stand green in a dress," he said, "Very unlucky!"

"Well how was I to know that she had saved my life?" exclaimed Frederick, some hours later, as he and Verity sat in the quiet refectory waiting for Adam to visit them, "Anyone who calls herself the Green Witch deserves to have perpetual bad luck in my book!"
"Shh..." replied Verity, "Walls have ears and her magic may be more potent in this holy place."
"I don't believe in witchcraft," said Frederick, stubbornly.
  Verity laughed.
"Much the same as I did not believe your tale of vampires when I first beheld you! We have a lot to learn, you and I. There is much in heaven and earth we do not comprehend!"
"I have said I am sorry," admitted Frederick, "The Green Witch can have anything I possess, by way of a gift, apart from my heart as that belongs to you."
"Yuk," replied Verity, thinking of the beating mass of blood and tubes on Frederick's chest a few hours ago.
"Well, thank you," Frederick pretended to be upset.

  An easy silence prevailed. Verity broke it with the much asked question,
"And you are sure you do not remember anything about where you have been or what has happened to you?"

  Frederick sighed but was very patient.
"As I have told you about ten times, I remember this huge pair of red eyes boring into my soul, then the soul-numbing pain of a bite and the world did indeed turn red. I then seemed to spend my days and nights begging for your return and feeling throttled by your love. Nothing else. It was all a bad dream until I woke and stepped over the Green Witch on the ground. But I stand by what I say...I do not like green in a dress!"
"You are incorrigible," replied Verity, giving his arm a playful push.

  Adam entered now in his brown habit and nearly wrung Frederick's hand off.

"It is good to see you as a man and not as that bloodsucking thing Lawrence brought here so many months ago," he told Frederick.
"Talking of Lawrence, where is he?" asked Verity.
"Sleeping, he said but I think he believes he is superfluous to requirements now Frederick is restored."
"He is a dear and loyal friend!" replied Frederick, "and as such he must be the best man at our wedding. Can you come, Adam? Can you leave the monastery?"

Adam shook his head.
"It is not possible," he admitted, "However I would be pleased and proud if you and Verity would accompany me to see my father and return the staff he gave Verity, as you never know if it will be needed again. Vampires, like bad pennies, have a habit of returning."

Later that day the three of them set out to visit old Mr Curlious, leaving Lawrence to pack up his things, ready to accompany the pair back to the northern moors. Scar's End would always be their home with Liddy and Jet, and from there the union would take place.

Verity had tried to reassure Lawrence that his friendship was needed now as much as ever and always would be.
"Where would Frederick or I be if it were not for you, Lawrence?" she told him when he had awakened from his slumbers, "I know you find our tale incredulous and you were not there to witness what happened when the Green Witch cast her spells but your friend...my fiancé... stands recovered before us both. Frederick will love you, Lawrence, in a way he will never love me and our gratitude to you can never be repaid. We want you to live with us at Scar's End and not worry about vampires any more. Will you do that?"

Verity looked at the man after her speech and was astonished to find tears coursing down his cheeks.
"Dear Lawrence," she said, "You brought Frederick and I together, as it were and we both want you in our lives..."

She gave the man a hug and heard him say in a small voice,

"If you will have me, I shall be honoured."
Peace had finally entered Lawrence's world and he saw a calm, quiet retirement ahead after the long, dark months of despair.

Two weeks passed slowly away and Frederick recovered strength and flesh and the difficult times he and Verity had faced now seemed a dim and distant memory. They returned to the northern moors and to Scar's End where Liddy was wild to see them and Jet was as excited as a cat can be. He raced round the parlour, knocking over vases and ornaments and the women ran around catching them whilst Frederick laughed.

Lawrence and Frederick lodged together to give Verity the space and time she needed to recover from the arduous journey and to plan the wedding. Liddy would be the maid of honour and Jet was to have a pink bow for the ceremony. "The vicar will not like a black cat in the church, Miss," Liddy told her, "He'll think the animal will jinx the service and your union!"
"We both know that is nonsense, Liddy, but, as this outdated belief seems to be common here, Jet can sit in the willow basket outside the church and wait for us. Be sure to find someone to take care of him and if he gets the least bit anxious then he is to be returned to the house."

Liddy promised to find a thoroughly reliable person to take care of him and the proceedings continued smoothly. Verity managed to gain a little weight so her figure would do justice to a long white dress and Frederick was fitted for a lavender coloured suit. Lawrence would look splendid in pale grey.

Two days before the union, Liddy came home and said she had gone to see Frederick for the last time before the wedding, and she happened to mention to Verity that he was going to try to eat some kidney for his supper, as he had been revolted by flesh and even more so by anything containing blood since the curse left him.

Verity was angry, she put on a cloak and hat, necessary as the day was cool and showery, and walked briskly until she reached her beloved's lodgings. She knocked on the door impatiently and Lawrence answered it.

"Ah, Verity, we were just going to partake of some supper so will you join us?"

In answer, Verity stormed through to the dining room and cast her disgusted eyes over the plates of meat on the table. Frederick avoided her eye and put down the fork he had picked up to consume the meal.

Verity drew herself up to her full height.

"There are some things that are more important to me than life itself, Frederick, and I am come to tell you I cannot marry you after all!"

Frederick's face fell.

"But why?" he asked, "Why, Verity?"

Verity pointed to the revolting dead flesh on his plate. "Have you eaten any of that, Frederick?" she asked.

By way of answer Frederick pushed the plate away and remarked that he still found dead flesh revolting. Verity smiled and turned to Lawrence, bringing him into the conversation too.

"Perhaps I was a little hasty," she admitted, "However I want a promise from you both that NO dead pieces of animal, bird or fish shall enter my house when you both come to reside there! ONLY Jet shall eat of what we call meat because that is his natural diet."

Lawrence raised his eyebrows but picked up both plates and transferred them to the kitchen without a word. Verity in full flow was not to be thwarted.

"Did you hear me, Frederick?" she asked, "Liddy told me you were preparing to consume dead flesh again!"

Frederick threw back his head and laughed.

"How I love your strong spirit and your views that cannot be argued with," he replied, kissing her flushed cheek.

Verity smiled.

"Then we understand each other very well," she said, "I went through hell on earth for you, Frederick, and now my house is going to be free from tortured souls of any kind!"

Her fiancé nodded and held out his hand.

"I have had enough of murder, blood and suffering to last me a lifetime," he told her, "I am more than happy to eat bread and vegetables and Lawrence will be more than happy to grow what we need now the blood vats and the vampires are no more! He is an excellent gardener when he has the time!"

Verity went home with a lighter heart and told Liddy that the men were not to be served dead flesh of any kind. "More than enough blood sucking has gone on here," she told the maid, "Now we usher in a new era of peace and that cannot be maintained if we bring in slaughtered souls who have equal rights with us to life."

Liddy nodded.
"As you say, Miss. As you say."

Once it was dark, Verity went and stood in her room, gazing down at the house front where she had first seen the bats. How long ago that seemed! In a day she would welcome her new husband to the house and they would settle down where her uncle had once been happy, before the curse came upon him.

"I commit your spirit to heaven, dear uncle, and to everlasting peace," she murmured, as the wind blew leaves against the windows in an autumn gale.

Later she went to bed to sleep deeply and dream of nothing more than being a wife and a mother to Jet. The spell of the bloodsuckers was broken and tranquillity had once more descended on Coombe Heights. No longer would the night ring out with weird screams and wails and village folk would be safe to wander abroad and leave their windows open in summer heat. The reign of the vampire, in Scar's End at least, was over.

CPSIA information can be obtained
at www.ICGtesting.com
Printed in the USA
LVHW042128241120
672607LV00021B/330